VICTOIRE

Also by Maryse Condé

VICTOIRE

My Mother's Mother

Maryse Condé

Translated by Richard Philcox

ATRIA INTERNATIONAL

NEW YORK   LONDON   TORONTO   SYDNEY

ATRIA INTERNATIONAL

A Division of Simon & Schuster, Inc.
1230 Avenue of the Americas
New York, NY 10020

This book is largely a work of fiction. Names, characters, places, and incidents are transpositions of the life of the author's mother and grandmother.

First Atria International hardcover edition January 2010

ATRIA INTERNATIONAL and colophon are trademarks of Simon & Schuster, Inc.

For information about special discounts for bulk purchases, please contact Simon & Schuster Special Sales at 1-866-506-1949 or business@simonandschuster.com

The Simon & Schuster Speakers Bureau can bring authors to your live event. For more information or to book an event, contact the Simon & Schuster Speakers Bureau at 1-866-248-3049 or visit our website at www.simonspeakers.com.

Designed by Jill Putorti

Manufactured in the United States of America

10   9   8   7   6   5   4   3   2   1

Library of Congress Cataloging-in-Publication Data is available.

ISBN 978-1-4767-8636-0
ISBN 978-1-4391-0058-5 (ebook)

For my three daughters
and
two granddaughters

Those who have helped me in this reconstitution are too numerous to mention. But I would like to thank personally Raymond Boutin, Lucie Julia, Jean-Michel Renault, and, in particular, Jean-Pierre Sainton.

What does it matter whether I remember or invent,
Whether I borrow or imagine.

—Bernard Pingaud,
Les anneaux du manège: écriture et littérature

VICTOIRE

Victoire

She died long before I was born, a few years after my parents were married.

All I have of her is a sepia-colored photo signed by Cattan, the photographer in vogue at the time. Set on top of the piano where I practiced my scales, the photo depicted a woman wearing a dress with a wide lace collar that gave her the look of a schoolgirl. An impression heightened by her slight figure. On her tiny feet were a pair of patent leather button shoes like those of a first communicant. A gold chain necklace was clasped around her delicate neck. How old could she have been? Was she pretty? I couldn't say. However, once she had captured your attention you couldn't take your eyes off her.

The sight of her never failed to make me feel uneasy. My mother's mother had that Australian whiteness for the color of her skin. Her soft-colored eyes like Rimbaud's, set deep in their sockets, were reduced to two Asian slits. She was staring at the lens without the shadow of a smile and without any attempt to appear gracious. Her headtie knotted with two points signified an inferior station. *Kité mouchwa pou chapo* (Swap the headtie for a hat) was the expression of the time that paid homage to a woman's social ascension. In short, she jarred with my world of women in Italian straw bonnets and men necktied in three-piece linen suits, all of them a very black shade of black. She appeared to me doubly strange.

One day, I must have been seven or eight, I couldn't keep it bottled up any longer.

"Maman, what was Grandmama's name?"

"Victoire Elodie Quidal."

The name filled me with admiration, especially as I lamented the sound of my own. I particularly loathed my first name, which I considered insipid. Maryse, little Mary? Her name resounded with the deep ring of a bronze medal. Resonant.

"What did she do in life?" I persisted.

I can remember dusk was falling and the sun was already an orange color in the sky that was veering to gray. We were in my mother's bedroom. Me, sprawled on her bed, although it was strictly forbidden. She, sitting next to the wide-open window to take advantage of the last rays of sunlight. With her finger elegantly encased in a silver thimble, she was pushing a needle as she darned.

"She hired out her services," she blurted.

"You mean she was a . . . servant?" I said, mortified in disbelief.

My mother turned to face me.

"Yes. She was a cook."

"A cook!" I exclaimed.

I couldn't believe it. My mother, the daughter of a cook! My mother, who had no palate and was notoriously incapable of boiling an egg. During our stays in Paris we would make do on weekdays scraping out cans of food, and on Sundays, we would scour the neighboring restaurants.

"A peerless cook," my mother emphasized. "She had the touch of a genuine chef."

Delighted, I hastened to add, "Me too, I'd like to be a cook."

Going by my mother's expression, I knew I was on the wrong track. She wasn't bringing me up to be a cook, not even a chef. I quickly changed the subject and made a diversion.

"And she didn't teach you anything, not even one recipe?"

She continued without answering the question.

"She first worked in Grand Bourg for the Jovials, some relatives of ours. That ended badly. Very badly. Then . . . then she migrated to La Pointe and hired out her services to the Walbergs, a family of white Creoles, right up till she died."

"That's where I grew up," she added.

I went from amazement to stupefaction. Reality was stranger than fiction. To think that this woman, my mother, who was a black militant before her time, had grown up with a family of white Creoles! How could this be? I tried to clarify matters.

"She never got married, then? Who was her father?"

Such a conversation might surprise some people. At the time, to have a father, to be recognized by him, to share his daily existence or quite simply bear his name, was the prerogative of a rare privilege. It was no shock to me that my parents, like so many others, emerged out of a kind of fog. My father, an unrepentant chatterbox, claimed that his father had gone to dig for gold in Paramaribo, Dutch Guyana, abandoning his mother, who was breast-feeding her baby on the Morne à Cayes. Other times he claimed his father was a merchant seaman, shipwrecked off the coast of Sumatra. Where did the truth lie? I think he re-created it at will, taking pleasure in enunciating the syllables that made him dream: Paramaribo, Sumatra. Thanks to him, from a very early age I understood that you forge an identity.

My mother folded her darning.

"I don't want to talk about all that just now. It's too painful. Another time, perhaps. Go and do your homework."

Petrified, I left the room.

Obviously, there never was "another time." We never resumed that conversation. My mother never revealed to me who her father was or the circumstances of her birth. Yet I could never get that conversation out of my head. It was probably then that I made the resolution to research the life of Victoire Quidal. But my own life has been so chaotic. I let the years go by. Sometimes I would wake up at night and see her sitting in a corner of the room, like a reproach, so different from what I had become.

"What are you doing running around from Segu to Japan to South Africa? What's the point of all these travels? Can't you realize that the only journey that counts is discovering your inner self. That's the only thing that matters? What are you waiting for to take an interest in me?" she seemed to be telling me.

Now I have the time to follow her footsteps.

Her picture is somewhat blurred and difficult to identify. For some, she was lovely. For others, pale and ugly. Yet others saw her as a downtrodden creature, illiterate and of no interest. And some as a real Machiavelli in a petticoat. When describing her, my mother would use those worn-out clichés of the Antilles that no longer mean anything.

"She could neither read nor write. Yet, she was the mainstay of the family, a formidable woman."

Certainly not! Certainly not the mainstay of the family. However, with her meager resources she managed to force open the doors of the burgeoning black bourgeoisie for her daughter.

But was it really worth it in the end?

That is the real question I ask myself. That ample faculty my mother had for suffering and torturing herself, which she left to all of us—Victoire was the cause. Thinking she was acting for the best, she condemned my mother to live her childhood in solitude and ostracism, which had a considerable influence not only on her character and behavior but also on that of her descendants.

I often wonder what would have been my relation to myself, my vision of my island, the Antilles and the world in general, what my writing that expresses all this would have been, if I had been cradled in the lap of a buxom, jovial grandmother, full of the traditional tales: Tim, tim! Bois sec! *Is the audience asleep? No, the audience is not asleep!*

A grandmother, former dancing star of the *gwo ka* and mazurka, whispering in my ear sweet myths of the past.

Such as it is, here is the portrait I have managed to trace, whose impartiality or even exactitude I cannot fully guarantee.

ONE

I n the hamlet of La Treille on the island of Marie-Galante, not far
from the town of Grand Bourg, the name of Quidal is as common as grains of sand on the beach. This is their domain. Rumor
has it that they are descendants of the property belonging to Master Antoine de Gehan-Quidal, owner of a sugar plantation. Ruined
after the abolition of slavery, he returned to France and left behind a
hundred or so "new citizens" in his slave cabins. The branch I come
from had nothing to distinguish it from the others. Just as black. Just
as famished. My great-grandparents were a strange bunch. Oraison,
the third son of Dominus, who, like his father and grandfather before him, cast and hauled up his fishing nets deep in the ocean, had
married, or rather lived with, his cousin Caldonia Jovial. They had
engendered a dozen children, five of whom still remained on this
earth. Their cabin was no different from the others. Built of pine-
wood and protected by sheets of zinc siding. No veranda. No cement
floor. Cooking and washing was done in the yard where a group of
male papaya trees grew. Oraison, a petroleum blue Negro, as long as
a day without bread, had a stock of tales that any qualified research
specialist would describe as "erotic." Fish were compared to the male
member, thick and sticky; seawater to the liquid that soaks women

down there. He also sang in a pleasant high-pitched voice. Although he was no professional, his singing talents were often called upon at wake ceremonies. As for Caldonia, she interpreted dreams. People came from far and wide to unlock their dreams.

"Caldonia? *Ka sa yé sa?*"

And she would coast confidently from one answer to the next: "Fish means mortality. A lost tooth, death. Pregnancy, good luck. A wound, bad luck. Blood on yourself, grief. Blood on others, victory."

One night, a dream bid her to take a closer look at the belly of her eldest daughter. Eliette, who was not yet fourteen, was pregnant. But Caldonia was quite pleased. Girls are meant to give birth. Better earlier than later. Eliette, however, made a great secret of it. She refused to reveal the name of her accomplice, so resolutely that Oraison ended up whipping her with his leather belt. She bore the lashes like a martyr, but still didn't open her mouth and kept mum. Her brothers and sisters described her sobbing at night and how at eleven o'clock every morning she would run to waylay the postman. Was she hoping for a letter, she who couldn't even read?

On Sunday, August 15, Caldonia was slipping on her best dress to attend mass when Elie came to warn her that his twin sister had lost her waters. The birth was not looking good. Her pelvis was too narrow. Seeing Eliette's blood gradually seep over the straw mattress, Martha Quidal, the midwife, had no choice but to send for Father Lebris, who at one thirty in the afternoon recited the prayer for the dead.

More than the sudden death of Eliette was the appearance of the newborn that shocked the family. A full head of thick black silky hair. Eyes the color of clear water. A skin tinted pink. For heaven's sake! Where did Eliette cross paths with a white man? There were no whites in La Treille. The only exceptions were the pallid priests barricaded against malaria, locked in their presbyteries. As for the plantation owners, most of them had deserted the sugar plantations for lack of profit. At one point there had been the soldiers of the fourth regiment garrisoned at Grand Bourg. Once they had experienced marching under the tropical sun, one-two, one-two, with knapsacks on their backs, they had gone back to France. Perhaps these were the ones who had wreaked havoc among the fair sex in their youthful ardor. Was that where we should be looking for the father?

For the time being, indifferent to these conjectures of the baby's paternity, all Oraison could think of was how they were going to get rid of this fateful object. The pond close to the rum factory or the cliff known as devil's leap? The latter was the perfect setting for creatures of this type. But the child raised its eyelids and stared at Caldonia. The science of motherhood had not yet been invented, but never mind, Caldonia was deeply moved by this silent exchange. Everything was decided in that one brief instant. A bond was tied that was only to become undone fourteen years later when Caldonia died from having eaten a banana in the heat of the midday sun. The little girl stole the heart of her grandmother, who had seldom experienced such feelings. Caldonia was God-fearing, but her soul did not exactly pine for Him. Her husband irritated her. Her children left her indifferent. From one day to the next, all that changed. She became devoted, possessive, demanding, and anxious. No egg was fresh enough, no breast of chicken white enough, and no flour light enough for the baby's stomach. To prevent diarrhea she mixed the baby's cereal with Hépar spring water. Quite unheard of! In a place like La Treille, where the children ran naked, with swollen bellies, reddish hair, and two slimes of mucus oozing out of their nostrils, this type of love seemed incredible. You had to respect it, though. They are still talking about it today.

The choice of first names was Father Lebris' decision. Victoire! Because in fact her birth was a victory. Poor Eliette had gone to join the dwelling place of the dead before she had lived her life, whereas her daughter testified to the glory of the Eternal in all His ways. Elodie! Because it was Saint Elodie on the calendar. Malicious gossip implied that Victoire's papa was in fact Father Lebris. Nothing was farther from the truth. God had given this Breton a calling when he was only eight years old. God was his rock and his fortress. As a seminarian he wrote psalms that his superiors deemed sins of pride. Did he think he was David? That's why as soon as he was ordained, they shipped him off to the Negroes on a godforsaken island in the very middle of the Caribbean.

On his arrival in Marie-Galante in 1870, barely twenty-two years after the abolition of slavery, he fell in love with this galette of an island that the sun cooked over and over again in its oven. The condition of his flock broke his heart. Freedom is an abstract concept, a dream of the affluent. As slaves, these men and women were less destitute. In their servitude, a master provided them with a roof over their heads and enough not to starve to death. As free men, what did they own except their poverty? If Father Lebris had lived, he would probably have been a mentor to Victoire, and perhaps her destiny would have been different. Unfortunately, she was not yet one year old when malaria triumphed. Like Eliette, he was laid to rest under the casuarina trees in the graveyard on the outskirts of Grand Bourg. For the second time, Victoire was abandoned. She remained in the hands of a woman who worshipped her, but who was illiterate and basically incapable of educating a child.

Around 1880, the migration from Marie-Galante began. The economists teach us that the emerging production of beet sugar in Europe began to destabilize the Caribbean market. From Saint-Louis, Capesterre, and Grand Bourg the inhabitants streamed toward the "continent" Guadeloupe, as they call it without a trace of irony. Their region of choice was Petit Bourg, where employment was to be had thanks to a factory and two rum distilleries. The sea too was bountiful: amberjack, sea bream, tuna, and snapper. You could fish with traps or dragnets. The newcomers pitched their cabins outside the town, in places today known as Pointe à Bacchus, Sarcelles, Bergette, Juston, and as far up in the hills as La Lézarde and Montebello. Elie had just set up house with Anastasie Roustain, known as Bobette, who had given him two sons. In order to feed his family, he decided to leave Marie-Galante and proposed taking with him his twin sister's daughter, whom he considered his own despite her unfortunate color.

Only Elie knew for certain who was Victoire's father. He had bad-mouthed her and flown into enough tempers in his jealousy! What did she hope to get from this white man? A soldier into the bargain. A soldier's like a sailor: instead of a woman in every port there's one in every garrison.

Caldonia refused categorically to let the apple of her eye go. What would her life be without the girl she idolized? Victoire was five or six years old. The sound of her voice was seldom heard. Nor was there hardly a smile, a ripple of laughter, or one of those cabriole dances that make childhood so delightful. It was as if her joie de vivre had been buried with her maman. Her hair was so straight and smooth that any braids became undone in minutes and flopped over her face, covering it with a silky curtain of mourning. In order to soothe her nightmares, Caldonia put her to sleep in her bed. Night and day, huddled against her grandmother, she acquired the bitter smell of her old clothes. The smell of sweat, dirt, and arnica.

At this time, the very poorest were preoccupied with an education. Free schooling for all had been one of Monsieur Schoelcher's promises, which they planned on keeping. The Brothers of the Christian Doctrine of Ploërmel had opened a school in Les Basses, where the airport now stands. Apparently, Caldonia didn't think for one moment of enrolling Victoire. No more than she did her younger children. As a result, my grandmother never learned to read or write. She never learned to speak French correctly, and so as not to shock her daughter's acquaintances, she kept a stubborn silence under all circumstances.

The only schooling she received—but can we really call it schooling?—was religious. Aurora Quidal taught catechism in her wattle cabin. Sitting in a circle, the children would chant, oddly alternating phrases in Creole and in French.

Ka sa yé sa: lanfé?

One God in three distinct persons.

Ki jan nou pé vinn pli bon.

Eat and drink. This is my body.

Throughout her life, Victoire, even though she never spoke of it, remembered her childhood as a paradise lost. It appears, however, that it was mostly dull, hardly entertaining, and darkened by poverty, which was the lot of the laboring classes.

The day would begin with the white light of dawn seeping through the commissures of the cabin's only window. Oraison and Elie, up in the dark since three in the morning, prepared a billy can of food, then went to join Oraison's brother before setting off to sea in the boat christened *Ezékiel*. One hour later Caldonia ventured out of doors. She emptied the *toma* of the night's urine, rinsed out her mouth, and said her prayers: a dozen Hail Marys and two Our Fathers. She lit the fire in the hearth, three rocks arranged in a triangle, and while the water was boiling, she would shake Lourdes, the youngest, to take Théodora the cow to the pond, and then woke Félix and Chrysostome.

Breakfast, if we dare call it that, was quickly expedited. Mother and children dipped their stale slice of *kassav* in some weak *tchòlòlò* coffee. Depending on the time of year, Félix and Chrysostome would go down to the cane fields or hoe the family's Creole vegetable garden while Lourdes, in charge of the household chores, would sweep the yard with a palm broom. Finally, Caldonia would enter the room where Victoire was sleeping. Then followed a long cuddling session that would have surprised a good many people. Where did Caldonia get this rosary of sweet talk from? These loving caresses? This fondling? She would carry Victoire to the water barrel. The water was cold. The little girl would whimper while her grandmother rubbed her dry and slipped on cotton panties that couldn't hide her protruding belly button. Then she did her hair. Victoire only found consolation once she had been given her cereal flavored with cinnamon and sweetened with wild honey. Then Caldonia would gather up the bundles of dirty washing collected from the town during the week. Ever since the time of the great plantation houses, the women in her family had been washerwomen, and they were proud of this skill that placed them above the common lot. Finally, she set off for the washhouse.

This washhouse, the one at La Croix, no longer exists today. It was built over a spring, now dried up, but once bubbling and joyful, called Espiritu. A dozen washerwomen would be up to their thighs in the water. There would be a babble of creole, laughter and cries amid the slap and beating of clothes mingled with the smell of *savon de Marseille* and the Sainte-Croix *eau de Javel*. For Caldonia, Victoire was the most adorable little girl in the world, a gift from the Good Lord who had been meager in His generosity. A photo that no longer exists today or perhaps never existed, but that I can re-create, does not allow us to throw further light on the matter.

It wasn't every day you had your portrait taken at La Treille. The photographer came from La Pointe with his magic box, his plates and black cloth. Oraison was dressed in his best suit. Black striped serge trousers. Jacket. Even a waistcoat. Bare headed. His badly combed mop of hair gives the final touch to his rustic look. Standing beside him, Caldonia is wearing her best Creole costume. Her madras headtie seems to me to be tied somewhat curiously. Its diagonal pleats are tight-fitting like a bonnet. The children are lined up in a row in front of the couple. In the center Victoire stands out like a chick among a brood of ducklings.

For most people Victoire was scary, with her skin too white and her eyes too light. A superstition coming from Nan-Guinnin claims that the souls of the dead, if they are lucky, manage to escape from the jars where they are held captive and slip into the bodies of children. Consequently, they reacquire the joy of living. This must have been the case for Victoire. She was one of the walking dead, a zombie. Sometimes she would grab a handful of guinea grass and chew on it. Most of the time her hands lay palms-up on her lap while she stared straight in front of her.

Others were convinced she was no less than Ti-Sapoti: that so-called orphan who haunts the roadside at night, dragging the passerby, who has the misfortune to stop and show compassion, into unknown regions. *An ba la tè?* No one knows where.

"*Ka ou ka fé là, ti-doudou an mwwen?*"

"What am I doing here?" Ti-Sapoti, dries his tears and becomes a predator.

When Caldonia had finished her washing, she crammed a *bakoua* hat onto Victoire and returned to La Treille. Lourdes had already put the root vegetables to boil and thrown in a hot pepper and a pig's tail. They would always eat in silence. After lunch, Caldonia pounded her starch, carefully grinding the lumps. Then she would starch her washing and hang it out to dry. After that, usually flanked by Victoire, she would go down to the shore and wait for Oraison's return. If she didn't immediately take charge of the proceeds from the fish he had caught, he would distribute three-quarters of the money to his string of girlfriends and drink the remainder with his *banélo* of buddies. Each time, this return to land was a ritual. Oraison's boat came into view on the horizon, made straight for the beach, then seemed to change its mind and head out for the open sea. Making a final skillful sweep, it would turn back toward the shore. It was then that the fishermen would jump into the waves and drag the boat behind them like a reluctant, untamed animal.

There came a softness in the evening air. The landscape imitated a picture postcard.

The sun drowned itself over by Dominica. With the irons laid on the burning coals of an outside stove, Caldonia would iron her washing after having smoothed it with candle wax. Oraison would be sucking on his pipe, while mending the mesh on his fish trap. Lourdes was simmering the thick soup. Félix and Chrysostome would be telling stories while roasting corn cobs that Victoire nibbled on. Oraison would often join in the conversation and come out with one of his half-invented stories that he was so good at.

Once, according to him, an orca had dragged in its wake the *Ezékiel* all the way to Antigua. Together with his brother and son, he had crossed the Grand Cul-de-Sac Marin, leaving behind them the white sand beaches of Saint-François. Suddenly the animal disappeared. However hard they scrutinized the deep blue surrounding them, all they could see were fishing boats like theirs. Another time they had passed a floating wreck of a ship loaded with men with slit eyes, lemon-colored skin, and black hair who pointed to them, babbling in a strange tongue. In the time it took to get their senses back, the ship had vanished. And then once, when they were far out in the ocean, they saw the water rise up like a mountain. The boat began to dance from one crest of a wave to the next. A few yards distant, a genuine wall of water was unfurling.

"An mwé!" they had shouted in despair.

Suddenly, as if by magic, the wall collapsed in a haze of drops and everything was back to normal, while the waves came to die softly on a line of reefs.

A pa jé! I'm not lying, the sea plays you some of the most incredible tricks!

Two

Once a month Caldonia, loaded with bundles of leaves, scrubbing brushes, and basins, rounded off her meager receipts from washing and fishing by scrubbing the floors of the mayor, Fulgence Jovial. He was her cousin twice removed, but he preferred to boast of his more flattering relationship to Jean-Hégésippe Légitimus, the first black man to have entered the political arena. He had been his right-hand man at Grand Bourg and, like him, proclaimed himself "Grand Nègre," an expression that has nothing to do with money but implies intellectual and human values, self-pride, respect, and social esteem.

After having knocked up half the girls who were at an age to be impregnated on the galette of Marie-Galante, Fulgence Jovial mended his ways and married at the town hall and church Gaëtane Sébéloué, the illegitimate daughter of a bastard mistress of a wealthy owner of a sugar plantation. Thanks to the estate of his wife, he could boast of owning the most precious of mahogany furniture in his upstairs-downstairs house. Like a guide in a museum, he would walk his visitors through one room after another, having them admire the wardrobes from Nantes, the chests of drawers, the consoles, and above all the magnificent sideboards.

When Caldonia went to work for the Jovials, she entrusted Victoire to her sister, a trinket seller at the market. On this particular day, she made an exception because for once Thérèse was in Grand Bourg. The Jovial couple had in fact an only daughter, Thérèse, whom they idolized. Going against Fulgence's wishes, who considered music frivolous and dreamed of her becoming a doctor, Thérèse was studying piano in Cuba under the great Marista Nueva Concepción de la Cruz and only returned once or twice a year to visit her parents. A few years earlier she had held Victoire at the church font, as she did dozens of children every time she came back to Marie-Galante. In our islands the godmother is chosen wisely; we can even say it's a calculated choice. She is a surrogate mother. Well-off, even very wealthy, she must be able to give her godson or goddaughter everything the biological mother cannot. And she should be capable of taking over in the event of death. Thérèse cared little for the numerous children she was supposed to have in her charge. But she had a particular liking for Victoire. Was it because of her unusual physique? She never forgot to bring her back a *recuerdo de Cuba,* however small it might be.

On this particular day, she had her come up to her room, a *bonbonnière* filled with her childhood toys: celluloid and porcelain dolls, cuddly teddy bears, wooden puppets, and a rocking horse. Then she placed a 78 record on the phonograph. As soon as the music started, Victoire drew close to the gramophone to touch it. She remained rooted to the spot, fascinated by the slow rotation of the record. When the melody stopped, she who was usually so gentle began to stamp her feet:

"Mizik! Mizik!"

Amused, Thérèse started up the phonograph again and the morning was spent listening to one record after another. At one o'clock, when Caldonia came up to fetch her, Victoire refused to go with her. Quite unusual for her, she squirmed and sobbed enough to break your heart all the way to La Treille, constantly murmuring the magic word:

"*Mizik!*"

How I would like to discover the melodies that gave Victoire these first emotions!

I know that Thérèse's ambition was to become a concert pianist. But fate decided otherwise. After her love life had been wrecked, she retired to France, where she sank into oblivion. What was she listening to that morning? Was it a suite for piano by Isaac Albéniz, who was to become her favorite composer? Was it a beguine or a *bèlè* from Martinique? Was it one of those Neapolitan rondos so dear to Nueva Concepción?

We shall never know.

What we do know is that from that day onward, her interest grew for this atypical goddaughter, who, strangely enough, seemed to share her musical tastes and who was so different from the local *bitako* bumpkins. She placed her under the formal protection of Gaëtane, making her mother swear that she would take care of Victoire's well-being. In short, Thérèse first treated Victoire with great indulgence, then later cast her as the very picture of deceitfulness.

But let us not get ahead in our story.

CALDONIA NEVER LEFT La Treille. The island where she was born and where she would die fully satisfied her. She therefore instructed her sister, who went to La Pointe once a month, to procure a music box. The sister bought from Abel Lhullier, rue Frébault, a small metal trapezoid box painted in white and decorated with a double frieze of blue flowers. When you turned the handle as far as it would go, it emitted a metallic melody: the habanera from *Carmen* by Bizet:

L'amour est un oiseau rebelle

This quaint object was found among my mother's personal belongings together with jewel boxes, mother-of-pearl fans, letters, and bills. It was an intriguing piece. Nobody could understand where it came from.

Victoire now possessed more than a toy: a fetish. From morning to night she would listen to her music box, singing softly to herself. She even slept with it. Sometimes, Lourdes teased her by hiding it. She would then cry so hard that Caldonia became angry and laid into Lourdes with all her might.

Victoire's early years were uneventful. I can only point to one incident that people called supernatural. It happened when she reached seven or eight in the middle of Lent during the month of March or April.

One afternoon, Caldonia had left Victoire asleep and gone down to watch over Oraison's sale of fish. When she got back there was no sign of Victoire in her *kabann*. Nobody answered her calls. Completely beside herself, she began by beating Félix, Chrysostome, and Lourdes for not watching her. Then the entire family set off in a search party, running along every path and track.

In fact, where was there to go?

In those days there were no "ogres" in Marie-Galante feeding on young flesh. Child molesters and kidnappers were unknown. There were no wooded spots on the island where a foolhardy child could play in all innocence. Nothing but the infinite glare of a jailer-sun where stunted savannas alternated with cane fields. The harvest had taken place three months earlier, but the young cane stalks were already budding and impenetrable. Who would ever dream of penetrating their dense foliage?

An idea flashed across Caldonia's mind like a poisoned arrow: the ponds, what about all those ponds on the flat island? She began to run from one to another, frightening the goats and the chameleons sleeping among the loose stones. Félix ran to warn his father, who was downing neat rum punches one after another at the Keep on Pouring rum store, to tell him that the little girl had disappeared. He stood up in a daze, his mind blurred by alcohol but conscious of the enormity of the misfortune, and joined the search party. As night fell, they lit *chaltounés* and the torches studded the dark like large glowing eyes.

Around eleven in the evening some of them gave up, thinking to themselves that Victoire had gone back home to hell. They found her in the graveyard at La Ramée, two miles from La Treille. La Ramée is a delightful graveyard by the sea where the dead rest wrapped in the blue linen shroud of the ocean. Each grave is marked with a border of conch shells. Victoire was asleep on her mother's grave, under the cross that bore the clumsy lettering:

ELIETTE QUIDAL

PASSED AWAY IN HER FOURTEENTH YEAR

God, how our mothers die young!

Awakened without a word, Victoire slipped her hand into Caldonia's and trotted off beside her. She never told anybody what had happened that evening. Caldonia plied her with questions: How did she manage to cover such a distance? Had someone guided her? If she had found the way all by herself, then she must have seen it in a dream. Victoire didn't say a word and Caldonia worried herself sick. Was it a sign that her mother was calling for her and that her short time on earth was drawing to a close? Yet the year ended and others followed. Without incident.

When Victoire was ten she passed her catechism exam after two attempts. She could therefore take her first communion. First communion has the formality of a wedding and the gravity of a rite of passage. It takes place one Sunday morning at the time of high mass. A procession of children dressed in identical white albs, in order to eliminate any discrimination, with fingers joined together on mother-of-pearl rosaries and the girls wearing crowns of artificial flowers in their hair, enter the church singing. They walk up to the altar in unison. Then the families go to enormous trouble to make sure there is the *chodo* cake at the reception.

A few months later Gaëtane Jovial asked Caldonia if Victoire could come and help her servant Danila. Caldonia hesitated before giving her approval. Not because there was no offer of wages. This was usual for this type of *restavek* job. The truth was that ever since the unexplained incident at the graveyard, she didn't like to be separated from her granddaughter. Victoire followed her everywhere, silently losing herself in the shadow of her ample silhouette. She finally accepted because she thought the child would gain experience and an education. Gaëtane, in fact, was simply and reluctantly obeying Thérèse, who urged her to do so in all her letters. Like Danila, she attached little importance to Victoire. Like the people at La Treille, both of them must have been scared of her. Danila managed the amazing feat of never saying a word to her during all those years of cohabitation, except for giving her orders:

"Fô ou fè . . ."

"Pa obliyé . . ."

"Atansyon!"

In fact, Victoire was treated like a pariah, like a slave at the Jovials. Never like a relative, not even a poor or disreputable one.

Sweep, dust, scrub the floor, beat the rugs, wax the furniture, shine the silverware, wash the sheets, boil and starch them with the shirts and the petticoats, as well as help in the kitchen—such was her lot. Every morning she started work at six and ended her day at seven, even eight. She would walk back to La Treille in the dark and, exhausted, slip into Caldonia's bed (Caldonia had now been totally abandoned by Oraison). Curled up against her grandmother, she pretended not to hear the roar of the wind over the sea, the gallop of the three-legged horse, the *Bête à Man Ibè*, around the cabin and the wails of all those *soukouyans* scouring the countryside, thirsting for the blood of humans. To reassure her, her grandmother would tell her stories or hum songs. The little girl especially liked a canecutter's song:

Zip, zap, wabap
Ma bel, ô, ma bel

LET'S FOLLOW HER little silhouette, rigged out in her unprepossessing clothes, tripping over her bare feet. She wore her first pair of shoes when she was almost sixteen, a present Thérèse brought back from Havana.

The road from La Treille runs down from a rocky hill, then, on reaching level ground, joins the one from Grand Bourg at a crossroads marked by mango trees and a twisted calabash tree. It then veers to the left and enters the town center. If you continue straight on you come to the town hall, the masterwork of Sylvain Tarpinius, a student of Ali Tur, and the smell of iodine grips you by the throat. Victoire emerged onto the seafront with its fully rigged sailboats lined up along the wharf. Perhaps influenced by Oraison's fantastic tales, she distrusted this blue expanse. Moreover, she would cross it with great caution only three times throughout her entire life. Nobody knows what lies beneath the ocean, now calm, now churned with waves. However, she liked the sea breeze and its refreshing smell of benzoin. She sat huddled at the end of the jetty, her head turned toward Dominica, sitting dog-shaped on the blue of the horizon.

Then she retraced her footsteps as far as the Jovials' house. Soon, she would be down on both knees washing and scrubbing the brick red flagstones on the sidewalk. When she came in, Danila, who was sipping her coffee as sweet as honey, didn't even trouble to greet her with a *"Bonjou! Ou bien dònmi?"* Taking some money from her blouse, she groused:

"Sé lanbi yo vlé manjé jodi-là, oui!"

Victoire obeyed and flew off.

Her trip to the market was her daily escape, her little moment of liberty in the tyranny of her hardworking days. Nobody on her back. She was particularly fond of lingering in front of the meat booths and never tired of watching the butchers in their leather aprons slicing the carcasses with their meat cleavers—*wham!*—handling the scale pans with their bloodied hands and throwing, kind fellows, liver scraps to the dogs who stuck their tongues out at passersby. It was a pleasure to rediscover in *Eloges* Saint-John Perse's same fascination for these brutal scenes:

" . . . and Negroes, porters of skinned animals, kneel at the
tile counters of the Model Butcher Shops, discharging a burden of bones and groans,
And in the center of the market of bronze, high exasperated
abode where fishes hang and that can be heard singing in
its sheet of tin, a hairless man in yellow cotton cloth gives a
shout: I am God! And other voices: he is mad!"*

In the kitchen, Danila assigned Victoire only the thankless jobs, such as beating the conch meat, extracting the crabmeat, scaling the fish with a pointed knife, plucking the fowl, skimming the soup, cutting and chopping chives and shallots, pressing the lemons, and, at a pinch, cooking the Creole rice. But by dint of spying on Danila, like a slave who, scared of being punished, learns to read in hiding, Victoire learned her first lessons, perfecting herself in secret.

---

*From *Eloges and Other Poems*, translated by Louise Varèse. New York: Pantheon
Books, 1956.

THREE

Caldonia received no warning of her death in one of those dreams she professed to know the key to.

The day she passed away was marked by none of those signs, none of those omens people recall emotionally much later. Nobody could say:

"That morning the wind blew so hard the zinc sheeting on the roof flew off. Soared right over the trees!"

Or else:

"At five in the afternoon the sun turned into a ball of fire and set the dead stump of the guava tree ablaze. Whoosh!"

No, it was a Thursday like any other. Cool, because we were in Advent, on the eve of Christmas. The flame trees had bartered their scarlet blossom for a robe of rustling maroon pods.

At the age of fifty-five, Caldonia was fit as a fiddle. Not a thread of white in her picky hair. Merely a hint of stiffness in her right knee, an early sign of arthritis that plagues our family. As usual, she got up at four in the morning and became engrossed in interpreting her dreams. Nothing serious could be noted and she went about waking up the family, leaving Victoire for last as usual. Victoire no longer dreaded the cold water and washed herself on her own, voluptuously baring her delicate, white adolescent body, so different from the mannish build of the other women in her tribe. Her breasts were scarcely visible. A thick tuft, lighter than her hair, barred her pubis. Caldonia did her hair, endeavoring with grips, barrettes, and pins to get control of this great mass dripping with oil. While raking her hair with the comb, Caldonia warned her against men. She talked a lot about them, these men, ever since Victoire had seen her blood a year earlier. She told her about their unfathomable wickedness. Their irrepressible treachery. Their fundamental irresponsibility. What she didn't have to put up with, with Oraison! At the age of sixty, hadn't he just given a belly to a young girl from Buckingham who thumbed her nose at her, right in the middle of church?

Victoire walked down to the town, did her tour of the jetty, and set off for work. Then on Danila's orders she went to the market, where she bought four pounds of pork. Shortly before lunch, while the sweet-smelling ragout was simmering on its bed of chives and bayrum leaves, Chrysostome rushed into the Jovials. He was stammering that Caldonia had dropped the banana she had been eating and collapsed. By the time he had dragged her onto her bed and looked for her *poban* of asafetida at the bottom of the chest of drawers where she kept her remedies, her heart had stopped beating.

The last straw for the inhabitants of La Treille, who were already ill-disposed toward Victoire, was her behavior regarding this unspeakable tragedy. In our islands death is a spectacle. Grief is not supposed to be mute. It must be accompanied by a ruckus of tears, cries, wails, reproaches, and imprecations against the Good Lord. Some people roll on the ground in despair. Others threaten to commit an irreparable deed. Every eye is swollen and red.

La Treille was nothing but lamentations. People who had never been exactly fond of the somewhat brusque and discourteous Caldonia, who had scarcely given her the time of day, were sobbing their hearts out as if they had lost a loved one. Whereas Félix, Chrysostome, and Lourdes manifested their grief as was customary, Victoire remained standing, dry-eyed. Paralyzed, she did not approach the bed where the deceased lay. Beside the bed Oraison lay prostrate, moaning and enumerating the merits of his companion. Oh no, this was by no means the day for making whoopee. But that didn't prevent him several weeks later from moving in with Isadora Quidal, to whom he gave six more children. At the age of eighty, he apparently fornicated like a young colt.

The undertakers didn't immediately seal the coffin and waited for those coming from Goyave, who had been notified by cablegram from the post office that opened in Grand Bourg at the end of 1880. At six in the morning, the day after his mother's death, Elie stepped off the sailboat *Plaît à Dieu,* totally stunned, for he had adored Caldonia. She hadn't exactly returned the favor, since according to her, he looked too much like Oraison and gave her bad memories.

"What is death?" Victoire kept asking.

There was nobody to answer her.

"Yesterday she kissed me. Today she's gone. Where did she go?"

Under the three o'clock sun, the funeral cortege set off. The choirboys sang in their high-pitched voices: "I believe in thee, my Lord." The priest, a fair-haired young man newly arrived from Cahors, stumbled in the searing heat, like Jesus on the road to Calvary.

After the funeral, they went back to La Treille to empty what was left of the Père Labat rum in the demijohns and patch up memories of the deceased. It only took one demijohn for them to metamorphose her into a first-class clairvoyant with her heart on her sleeve. Hadn't she elucidated hundreds and hundreds of dreams for the distressed? Hadn't she, one Lent, taken in a wounded dog who was dragging herself along on three legs, whom everyone took for a neighbor transformed by magic and shouted "Shoo!" at? Above all, hadn't she showered with affection this "worthless dreg," this hardhearted Victoire who hadn't shed a tear over Caldonia's dead body?

All in all, it was a wonderful wake. When the inhabitants of La Treille split up at dawn, the men emptying their bursting bladders against the trees and bawling *"Faro dans les bois,"* they had the conviction of having accomplished that duty owed to each and every one of us at the end of our lives.

FROM THAT DAY on Victoire slept in town at the Jovials.

A mattress stuffed with vetiver was thrown down in the attic. As a result, she practically never went back to La Treille, where, except for Lourdes, nobody regretted her absence. From time to time Lourdes called in to inquire about her health and reel off tittle-tattle of very little interest. Who had given a belly to whom. Who had left whom for whom. Who had beaten whom. Who had dropped dead. Who had been born. And born with a caul, that one, a genuine net tight over his forehead. And consequently, capable of deciphering what the future held.

On Sundays, after mass, when Victoire could have enjoyed a little rest, Fulgence entertained his guests. All whom Guadeloupe counted in the way of socialist politicians braved the stretch of water to sit at his table. These receptions were a constant subject of discord with Gaëtane, whose Christian austerity was shocked by all this opulence. During their forty years of life together, it wasn't their only bone of contention, mind you. As a loyal follower of Légitimus, Fulgence liked to think of himself as a free thinker, member of the Sons of Voltaire Society, whereas Gaëtane was a religious nut, if you'll pardon the expression. These meals lasted virtually all day. In his shirtsleeves, Fulgence uncorked bottle after bottle of Saint-Emilion, Château Lafite, Château Margaux, while in champagne he had a particular liking for Ruinart. As for Gaëtane, her confessor allowed her just one glass of curaçao from Holland. Danila and Victoire would fly from the kitchen to the dining room, trays loaded with black pudding, whelks, stuffed clams, crab pâtés, conch *vols-au-vent,* and avocado salads. Not forgetting the entrées: *bébélé, colombo, calalou,* fish court bouillon, and other delights of Creole cuisine.

The banquet on Sunday, January 1, 1889, reached unheard-of heights. They made it into a feast fit for a king, as the saying goes.

The prodigal daughter, Thérèse Jovial, had finished her piano studies at last, and after six years in Cuba had returned home to live with her parents.

Let us sketch a portrait of Thérèse Jovial. Supple and sweet as a sugar cane stalk, she was extremely well proportioned, with a wasp waist that her father likened to a Tanagra figurine. She had an impish nose, a pair of languid eyes, and cheeks covered in elegant freckles. There was but one dark side to this engaging portrait. Her color. Yes, her color. Thick black. Tar black. Irremediable. She inherited it, this blackness, from Fulgence, since Gaëtane was very light skinned. As a result, those who were jealous of her nicknamed her Kongo. Or even more vulgarly, *bonda à chodiè*. This feature might explain why at the age of twenty-six she was still unmarried. Of course, the skeptics will retort that in those days black skin guaranteed legitimacy and, consequently, success with the masses. But politics is not aesthetics. For the young girl her color constituted a handicap. In Havana, the guitarist Eduardo Sandoval would have loved to play a duet with her for the rest of his life. Alas, he belonged to a bunch of mulattoes and his family put a holà to it.

The spoiled ways of an only child were tempered by an extreme grace. Thérèse spoke French with a lisp, which had a certain charm to it. Her Spanish was faultless. Like her Creole. Imitating her father, she wasn't ashamed to speak it or at times make it rhyme. In short, once again it was a shame no suitor came to claim this treasure.

Thérèse had stepped off the sailboat in Grand Bourg shortly after Christmas Day with three trunks of Spanish leather stuffed as usual with presents: an embroidered shawl for her mother, a Panama hat for her father, and a pair of lovely red pumps for Victoire. Victoire had never worn shoes in her life. Up till then, she had walked barefoot along the stony paths. Her soles were rough and cracked. Her nails gray and sharp like clam filings. Her toes pointing like the eyes of a crab. Nevertheless, she managed to slip on her red pumps. *Maché kochi. Maché kan memn.* Thérèse, who was enamored of harmony, was saddened by Victoire's wardrobe, two smocks made of jute. She had tailored for her two maid's aprons, made of black serge and edged in white, three loose-fitting *golle* dresses, as well as a Creole matador costume in dark green and mauve satin with an apple-colored headtie for high mass. Nobody could understand why Thérèse showered these acts of kindness on Victoire, who became no more affable with time. What a contrast! One slender and dressed in the latest fashion with a moleskin hat. The other looking no more than thirteen at the age of sixteen; a sloppily tied madras headscarf cut low across her forehead level with her pale eyes. She never smiled and walked woodenly, like a carnival *bwa bwa*.

Apart from these sartorial modifications, Thérèse's arrival changed little with regard to Victoire's condition at the Jovials. Each of them kept to the place assigned by destiny. There was no familiarity between godmother and godchild. Under her frigid appearance, Victoire must have been devoted to Thérèse as if she were the Blessed Sacrament herself. And Thérèse let herself be worshipped with a smug indifference. I have no knowledge of any conversation or exchange of words between them on any subject whatsoever.

As for me, there is one thing I find hurtful. Thérèse, who boasted she was a militant feminist and who had read Mary Wollstonecraft in the Spanish translation, never thought of teaching her protégée to read and write. If she had, she would have removed her from the obscurantism in which Victoire lived all her life. She would have opened the doors to another future for her. We can even imagine that her entire existence would have changed. It was not for want of opportunities, however. At the time, the Brothers of Ploërmel dispensed free evening classes for adults. In short, relations between the two girls were extremely limited. Victoire was responsible for bringing up the breakfast tray at nine o'clock on the dot, since Thérèse was graced with the adolescent faculty of sleeping late. If she had been left to her own devices, she would have slept until noon, something that is unchristian. Victoire would bring the sweet, fragrant coffee from Cuba that Thérèse was fond of. Papayas, guavas, and Bourbon oranges cooling on crushed ice. She would come up to the bed and whisper timidly:

"Ninnainne, lévé."

Thérèse would stretch catlike in her light brown colonial medallion bed made of locust wood, sit up amid the tangle of fine linen sheets, smile, and dismiss Victoire with the wave of her hand. And that's as far as it went.

Unlike La Pointe or Saint-Pierre in Martinique, Grand Bourg could boast of neither a theater nor a concert hall. Every Tuesday, Fulgence, Gaëtane, and their friends, who made up the embryo of a local bourgeoisie, gathered in the living room to listen to Thérèse. For them she would play just a few simple pieces: a little Chopin, sometimes some Liszt, not too virtuoso, or else The Carnival of Venice and The Siege of Saragossa. Victoire, instead of serving the guests the bowls of coconut sorbet and homemade cookies, braved the furious looks of Danila and had the nerve to go and sit behind a potted palm and listen in ecstasy to the flow of music.

The high point of these private concerts was when Thérèse played the Cantos Flamencos, anonymous gypsy ballads she had adapted for the piano.

FOUR

O n January 1, 1889, when thirty-four loyal Légitimus followers sat down to lunch, Fulgence introduced his protégé, the new elementary school teacher at Les Basses. Dernier Argilius, the youngest and last son of a poor farm laborer's family from Saint-Louis, bore his name, since his parents wanted the Good Lord to know that finally they had had enough. After fourteen children, and four who had died, they no longer wanted His heavenly gifts. Dernier was one of the first holders of the colonial diploma and a member of the Republican Youth Committee. It was rumored he was a former Légitimus party militant, a *zambo*. After the elections he had apparently been seen patrolling the streets and brandishing a stick, threatening people with light skins. There is a photo of him in a book by Jean-Pierre Sainton, a Guadeloupean historian. The requisite very black skin, a head of thick, frizzy hair curling over a domed forehead, a determined look, a broad nose, clearly drawn lips, and dressed in a tight-fitting frock coat. His expression is arrogant and mocking. *On bel nèg!* as the saying goes. Women devoured him with their eyes, lingering surreptitiously over the treasure that fitted tightly in his impeccable woolen trousers.

He wrote editorials in Légitimus's broadsheets. I discovered one: "We are hungry, we are thirsty, we are barefoot, we have no work;

we have no home, we survive thanks to the grace of God. Our families are impoverished. Our women have lost their beauty, bruised under the heel of destitution."

My reason for reproducing this piece of grandiloquent prose at the risk of boring my reader is because I would like to ask a question that I deem important. Dernier Argilius has gone down in history like Jean-Hégésippe Légitimus as an ardent defender of the illiterate oppressed Negroes emerging from the belly of slavery. When he died tragically in 1899, the entire island went into mourning. Ever since then, theses, monographs, and biographies have been written on the subject of this role model and martyr. My question, then, is what is an exemplary man? Is it only his writings, his public speeches, and his gesticulations that count? What weight does his personal life and private behavior carry? Dernier Argilius took advantage of I don't know how many women, wrecked the life of at least one of them, and engendered I don't know how many bastards who grew up without a father. Doesn't that count?

From the very minute Thérèse's and Dernier's eyes met, sparks flew that set their bodies on fire. During lunch he drew up a chair to her left and whispered pell-mell all the clichés of a miserable childhood, a humiliated adolescence, and a passion for the Race from a very early age. During dessert, she sat at the piano and accompanied him as he thundered out with his bass voice the old political favorites; all the guests joined in with a frenzy exacerbated by the alcohol ingurgitated:

> Nou voyé on blanc alé
> I pa fè annyen ban nou
> Voyé on pwèmyé milat
> I pa fè annyen ban nou
> Voyé on dézyèm milat
> An nou voyé Léjé alé pou I défann no z'entéré
> An nou voyé Léjé alé pou I monté o Pawlèman!

In the meantime, their blood was boiling with excitement. They were soaked with the burning sweat of desire. If they had been free to do so, they would have rushed into Thérèse's bedroom and, flouting bourgeois preliminaries, gone into action. Instead, they had to wait one long week, the time it took to elude Danila's vigilance and especially that of Gaëtane, who would be constantly warning her daughter:

"Pa ti ni konsomasyon san bénédisyon." (No consummation without a benediction).

Dernier, however, was not entirely blinded by passion, if passion there was. He devised a project that was approved by the party cadres and comrades in La Pointe with whom he corresponded regularly. Together with Thérèse, he would be in charge of an association that aimed at teaching political awareness to the laboring masses on Marie-Galante by way of the arts. He proposed calling it "A Call to the Arts, Citizens." Thérèse preferred "A Call to the Arts, New Citizens." But Dernier thought the adjective useless, even redundant, and his decision prevailed. Literary nights, poetry evenings, and music recitals were held one after another in the newly painted town hall, but apart from the usual handful of Fulgence's and Gaëtane's friends, it remained hopelessly empty.

For the festival of Sainte-Cécile, Thérèse managed to have the philharmonic orchestra shipped over from La Pointe. The forty-three musicians in their blue and white uniforms and white helmets lined up in front of the town hall and played to perfection excerpts from Meyerbeer's work. Apart from a few ragged urchins chewing on *grabyo koko* candies, not a peasant, farm laborer, fisherman, or worker took the trouble to turn up. Thérèse was so mortified she agreed to go along with Dernier, who suggested they concentrate their efforts on the school. At least there the audience is captive. The school principal, M. Isaac, an uptight mulatto, had hardened prejudices, but he feared Légitimus's people and complied with every request.

Thérèse and Dernier then decided to form a choral society. Unfortunately, they were unable to come to an agreement. As a feminist, lest we forget, Thérèse insisted on including women's voices and singing the famous "Hallelujah" chorus from Handel's *Messiah*. Dernier, who was against mixing the sexes, was all for teaching the same songs that the socialists sang in the Workers Chorale in La Pointe.

Marie-Galante, however, was impatient to hear about their engagement.

Some indiscretions had revealed their affair. It's true the lovers hid nothing. They galloped on horseback across the island to their trysts, Thérèse's butt strapped tight into an old pair of her father's trousers and her hair straightened with a hot iron and held in place by a net. They would meet in a cabin belonging to one of Dernier's brothers. In order to make up for its modest surroundings, Dernier had brought in a bed made of locust wood and an oval mirror in which it was whispered the couple gazed at their reflection before the act of penetration. Despite all that, people were understanding. Firstly, because the sin of love is not a sin. And then putting Easter before Lent is no crime! Who hasn't committed it? In fact, what marriage can claim to have escaped concubinage or *béni-rété*? The young girls who hoped to be bridesmaids had selected their gowns from the Printemps catalog. Others got help from dress patterns. Thérèse, an artist to her fingertips, drew her wedding dress on sheets of ecru paper and showed the sketches to her mother's dressmaker, who shook her head, helpless.

"An pé'é jen pé!" (I could never manage that.)

Against all expectations, on December 23, 1889, Dernier Argilius slipped onto the steamer for La Pointe. A little surprised, Thérèse, however, did not worry inordinately about this trip. She knew he loathed celebrating Christmas in the Catholic manner. Like his political mentor, he dreamed of combining December 24 with the anniversary of the death of Victor Schoelcher, combining the savior of the black race with the liberator of the Jews. She only began to suspect the truth when some good souls came to inform her that Dernier had emptied his house in Les Basses of all his papers, clothes, and, above all, the books in his library. Utterly distraught, she ran over to Monsieur Isaac, who confirmed that Dernier Argilius had left Marie-Galante for good, and good riddance! At the request of Jean-Hégésippe Légitimus, he had turned his back on teaching to devote himself entirely to journalism. Later on he was to become director of the newspaper *Le Peuple*.

Thérèse went down on both knees to beg Fulgence—the outraged father who threatened to write straightway to Légitimus to tell him of his protégé's unspeakable behavior—to remain silent. She reminded him that there had never been a promise of marriage in the true sense of the term. When she finally managed to get him to promise to stay put, she swallowed a whole bottle of what she thought to be arnica. In actual fact it was a purgative that Gaëtane had concocted with cassia and castor oil. Her entire body became inflamed. She defecated for a whole week and almost died: dehydration, sudden drop in blood pressure, and everything else. She regained consciousness only to be blinded by a photo on the front page of *L'Emancipation*: Dernier Argilius piously leading a pilgrimage to the Schoelcher museum, inaugurated with great pomp two years earlier, in front of a crowd of ecstatic workers. She fainted once again. After a month, she came through, but was so weak that Léonora Bilé, a Congolese, skillful in the art of herbs, came every day from Trianon to massage her wasted body with coconut oil macerated in balata bark.

It's a common fact that misfortune never comes singly. Thérèse was gradually recovering from this abominable desertion when they discovered that Victoire, who as usual never said a word, never divulged a thing, was hiding a belly under her shapeless *golle* dresses. Danila, who had been spying on her for weeks, had noticed that she no longer washed her bloodstained rags once a month. To be honest, she had been nurturing deep down an unspeakable intuition. When she confided her suspicions to Gaëtane, the latter expressed her doubts. Didn't Victoire take communion every Sunday at eight o'clock mass? Would she dare commit such a mortal sin? In order to back up her accusation, Danila had to force the unfortunate Vic-

toire to bare the still modest yet incomparable calabash of a belly
with a darker stripe down the middle and topped by an enormous
tumbler of a belly button.

Pregnant!

For whom? By whom?

Like Oraison with Eliette seventeen years earlier, Fulgence was
called to the rescue from his office at the town hall and unbuck-
led his belt. Victoire was less resilient than her mother. After five
bloody lashes on her shoulders, she let it out, the name that Danila
had not dared pronounce.

Thérèse fell into a swoon.

NOBODY WILL EVER know anything about the relations my grandmother Victoire had with Dernier Argilius.

That story has been erased. Deleted from memory. But I want to
know.

I want to know how they communicated their desire, where they
met and how many times. How did they manage to hide on an island
where nothing is secret? Was Victoire pregnant straightaway? What
drove her to him? Did her chaste adolescent heart become inflamed
at first sight during that famous New Year's lunch? Didn't she have
any consideration for her godmother, Thérèse, whose passion for
Dernier was common knowledge? Or did she want to take revenge
on her arrogance? Years later Thérèse told some close friends:

"Despite everything I did for her, she was always jealous of me. I
could see that in her eyes, but I never took her seriously."

She claimed that Victoire never felt anything for Dernier. All she
was looking for was a man of standing, "a valid father." She called
her an ungrateful wretch, calculating and manipulating. I don't believe a word.

As for Dernier, nobody will ever know why the man who possessed the most desirable young girl on Marie-Galante bedded also

one of the most destitute. Nor why he turned his back on both of them at the same time.

I can therefore only use my imagination.

It wasn't rape; that I'm certain of.

For her future son-in-law, whose heart she wanted to win through his stomach, Gaëtane used to send over a series of small dishes. At noon Danila would pile the plates on a tray that she covered with an embroidered napkin. With the tray on her head Victoire would trot off to Les Basses, which was then a densely populated suburb on the outskirts of Grand Bourg. She never found Dernier at home. He could be found either at the schoolhouse helping out the dunces, or downing neat rums at the Rayon d'Argent rum store with the party's farm laborers. She would push open the door, which was never locked (in those days a burglary was unheard of), and arrange the plates on the table. That too was a moment of liberty that she made the most of. In order to comply with his political opinions, Dernier lived in a modest two-room cabin. The place, however, was unique. Books! Piles of books! Everywhere you looked. Piled up on the floor. Stacked haphazardly on shelves along the walls. Some were dog-eared. Others were annotated. Yet others were in shreds. You sensed that their owner loved them and read them. Not like Fulgence, who kept his leather-bound volumes in a mahogany glass cabinet and never touched them.

What a magical object a book is! Even more so for someone who can't read, who doesn't know there are bad books that are not worth sacrificing whole forests for.

Victoire would turn them over and over again in the palms of her hands. Sometimes she opened them and studied the signs that were indecipherable to her. She regretted her ignorance. Yet her heart did not hold Caldonia to blame. All she wanted to remember was Caldonia's tenderness. Living a life of solitude, she could constantly hear Caldonia's grumpy, affectionate voice repeating the riddles whose answers she knew by heart but pretended to search for:

"*On ti bòlòm ka plin on kaz?*" (A little man who fills the whole room.) A candle.

One day. The heat was suffocating. Dry lightning streaked the sky. The sea was glowing like a gold bar being smelted. With tongues hanging out, the dogs did little else but sniff one another's backside and seek the shade. Livid, the anole lizards puffed up their dewlaps on the stems of the hibiscus. Victoire arrived at Les Basses soaked in sweat. For once, Dernier was at home. He had taken off his frock coat and, shirt wide-open on his hairy chest, he was fanning himself with a newspaper. She greeted him shyly in a muffled, slightly hoarse voice.

"*Ben l'bonjou, misié!*"

He inspected the tray, tasted the food, made a face, shrugged his shoulders, and exclaimed in Creole:

"What bunch of heartless individuals sent you out in this heat?"

Victoire remained expressionless. Did she share his opinion? He disappeared into the bedroom and came back with a towel that he threw at her.

"Go and wash your face in the washroom," he ordered.

"Washroom" was a fancy word for it. A trellis fence marked out a space behind the cabin where a half-empty water jar and toiletry utensils could be found. Victoire obeyed and went outside. He came out onto the doorstep to stare at her with his arrogant eyes. Out of modesty she hesitated to undo her headtie in front of him. When she finally made up her mind, her black hair immediately tumbled down to her shoulders.

"What's your name?" he shouted.

"*Victwa, misié!*"

"Where're you from?"

"La Treille, yes!"

She filled a basin, washed her face and neck, dried herself, then went back inside. He had settled back in the rocking chair and looked up to stare at her with sustained attention, caressing her breasts with his eyes. Under this fiery gaze, she picked up the dishes from the day before and got ready to take her leave.

It was then that he stood up and walked over to her.

"You're in too much of a hurry!"

He took her by the arm.

Did they make love that day? It's unlikely.

I believe on the contrary that she was frightened; frightened by his touch, by this male smell that was filling her nostrils for the first time. She wriggled free, secured the tray on her head, and made a bee line for the town. People who saw her shoot past strained their necks. What was this crazy girl running after? Sunstroke, that's all she could hope to get.

Danila's suspicions were aroused from the very first day. Monstrous suspicions. Amid the ensuing misfortune, she grouched that her heart had warned her before everyone else.

She was putting the final touches to a sea urchin stew when Victoire came charging in, red and sweating. She was coming back from Les Basses, Danila remembered. What was she running away from? No use asking her, she wouldn't answer. Danila noticed her hands trembling as she clumsily put away the plates she had brought back, even more awkwardly than usual. She almost fell flat on her face while crossing the yard. In charge of seasoning the salad, she mixed up the salt and pepper servers. While clearing the table, she crossed the knives and forks under Gaëtane's very eyes and earned a sharp reprimand to which visibly she paid no attention.

Then she left untouched her more modest meal (no hors d'oeuvres or dessert), which she took with Danila in the kitchen. She sat daydreaming, her chin resting on the palm of her hand, before tackling the washing-up and breaking two ramekins in one go.

ONE MORNING, SHE who was generally mute as a blowfish, started humming a song while putting the wash to bleach. An old wake ceremony song that Oraison used to sing at La Treille, each time accompanied by bursts of laughter that flew from all sides. An old melody that Caldonia liked:

> *Zanfan si ou vouè*
> *Papa mò*
> *Téré li an ba tono la*
> *Sé pou tout gout*
> *Ki dégouté*
> *Y tombé an goj a papa*

In her amazement, Danila, who was busy kneading the batter for vegetable marinades, grated her left middle finger, mistaking it for a chunk of pumpkin.

IF PEOPLE HAD eyes to see—but people are blind, that's a fact, and can't see farther than the end of their noses—they would have noticed one thing: that Victoire's beauty, up till then questionable, argued over, even contested, burst into the open.

Here she was suddenly less sickly, less adolescent. Not in the least bit little Miss Sapoti. A head of hair as thick as the Black Forest. Surreptitiously, her portliness made her breasts heavier and rounded her shoulders. Her overly pale complexion took on a velvety texture and darkened.

Danila, made perspicacious by her hatred, was the only one to notice this metamorphosis, which was even more suspect since Victoire no longer touched her food. What nurtured her were the kisses, the caresses, and the sweet words breathed into her. From where?

From a man, no doubt.

There is nothing like love to make a woman as beautiful as that. It's not only the feeling. But the act. Making love.

What man are we talking about?

Danila refused to imagine the unimaginable or a fortiori speak the unspeakable. As her nurse, *mabo* Danila had held Thérèse over the baptismal font. She had wiped her behind, washed her menstrual-stained undergarments. She had no proof whatsoever, but wanted to shout at her:

"Watch out! Open both eyes! You think she's a child, but she's not the child you think she is. She's a perverted little thing. A female of the first degree!"

Fifty years later, on her deathbed, Danila was still racked by remorse. She beat her breast: "Mea culpa, mea maxima culpa." For hadn't she heard whisper that Dernier was an incurable womanizer? Under the guise of literacy lessons, Dernier received a constant stream of peasant girls. Some rumors had it that he was the father of Marinette's son, who worked at the Folle-Anse plantation, and also Toinette's, who toiled at Buckingham. Yet she hadn't told anyone of these rumors. Not even her confessor. What was holding her back? The fear of hurting her beloved Thérèse. And now look what happened!

Her heart had jumped, that's for sure. But in the end, what purpose had it served? Nobody had come out of it unscathed and she had not protected the girl she worshipped.

WHAT DISGUSTS ME in all this is that Victoire was never considered a victim. I can excuse Thérèse, who was blinded by her own grief. But as for the others, there was not a moment of compassion. Victoire was just sixteen. Statutory rape. Dernier was twice her age. He was educated, and a respected, even well-known notable. Everyone treated her like a criminal. I like to think that she hid her tears in her attic, revolted by her pregnancy, but not complaining, crushed by her solitude and convinced of her insignificance. Perhaps too she was expecting Thérèse to say something, but she never did.

"Here we are the two of us, both taken for a ride. At least you carry the future in your womb. Me . . ."

Fulgence demanded Oraison come and take back his daughter. She had disrespected the sanctity of his home. Oraison turned up at eight in the morning—he hadn't gone to sea that day—flanked by Lourdes. Informed of her crime, he flung himself on Victoire and gave her such a slap that she fell to the ground, her mouth covered in blood. He then vented his anger by kicking and punching her. Under the terrified gaze of Gaëtane, Fulgence had to hold him back.

If he wanted to kill his child, let him do it elsewhere. There would be no bloodshed on his floor.

Without a farewell, without a thank-you, and, most significantly, without a penny, Victoire left the home where she had toiled for over six years, hugging the wicker basket containing the loose *golle* dresses and matador robe that Thérèse had forgotten to take back.

Poor Thérèse was in agony. Her monogrammed sheet pulled up over her head, she had been weeping and sobbing since the day before. She refused to open her door to Gaëtane, who was primarily concerned with the humiliation.

"Oh my goodness! People will laugh at us."

"Oh Lord! How will I be able to look at people at high mass?"

"Jesus, Mary, and Joseph, mercy on us!"

Thérèse did let Danila in; she was carrying a woman weed herb tea. Thérèse took the cup with trembling hands.

"*I pati?*"

Danila nodded that Victoire had left and there followed a long, uncomfortable moment.

Two months later Thérèse booked a category two first-class cabin on board the *Louisiane,* a steamship belonging to the Compagnie Générale Transatlantique. With no regard for her parents' grief, whom she was never to see alive again, she journeyed to France, where she lived for the rest of her life. Something was broken inside her. She had lost her savoir-faire and her assurance. She bought a two-bedroom apartment on the rue Monge, opposite the Lutetia amphitheater, and earned a mediocre living by giving music lessons to children of the colored bourgeoisie. Accompanying herself on the piano, she would hum the well-known melody that was still very topical:

J'ai pris mon coeur, j'ai donné à un ingrat,
A un jeune homme sans conscience
Qui ne connait pas l'amour
Ah! N'aimez pas sur cette terre
Quand l'amour s'en va, il ne reste que les pleurs!

She kept quiet about that period of her life. As a rule, seated at the piano, she would sum it up thus with her sweet, broken voice:

"I nursed a viper in my bosom and it bit me. My life is over. That's all I can say."

Sometimes between scales she became worked up and asked in a tone of despair:

"Why? Why me? I did nothing to deserve such a blow dealt by fate. I was pure. A virgin. Naive."

She never married.

ORAISON WAS WALKING in front, his chest puffed out in anger. Wretched females whose bellies bear nothing but shame upon shame! Behind him came Victoire and the sympathizing Lourdes. On leaving the town, where the Maurice Bishop Center now stands, Lourdes linked arms affectionately with her niece, who nestled against her side. Unfortunately, at that very moment, Oraison turned round and caught their gesture of affection. He sent them both flying, one to the right, the other to the left. Victoire lost her balance, fell into the ditch, and twisted her ankle. Thank God, her baby was unharmed.

In the space of a few years, La Treille had undergone major changes. Half of its inhabitants had emigrated to the mainland of Guadeloupe, leaving their cabins to go to ruin. Cut grass and sensitive plants filled the once Creole gardens. The trees were overgrown with creepers. The white blossom of the Santo Domingo briar rivaled the lilac flowers of the gliricidia. No longer were there oxen grazing under the hogplum trees. No longer any oxcarts, arms lowered, waiting to be loaded. There reigned an atmosphere of desolation. When Oraison had been in such a hurry to move in with Isadora, Félix, Chrysostome, and Lourdes had not tolerated the insult to the memory of Caldonia. In unison they moved to a cabin at the other end of the hamlet. Then Félix and Chrysostome each set up house with a woman and went their separate ways. Since Félix was Victoire's godfather, that was where Oraison brought the criminal, throwing her at his feet with a kick. Félix had given Victoire her baby formula; he had given her piggybacks and carved oxcarts from an avocado pit. Victoire was not the first and would not be the last to push in front of her the belly she got on credit. It was a mode that was here to stay, and stay for a long time, that's for sure. Deep down in his heart, Félix believed she should be spared. Blame should be placed above all on the wickedness of these Grands Nègres, these sermonizers, who were no better than the small-time blacks, even the maroons. But Destinée, his companion, couldn't put up with this slut under her roof and he had to give in.

Lourdes asked for nothing better than to inherit Victoire. But money was cruelly lacking. How could she feed yet another mouth? After much reflection, they came up with an idea.

Up till then, Victoire had escaped the bondage of working in the sugarcane fields. Now it was the only way out. Since she had never handled a hoe or a cutlass, she would offer her services as a cane bundler. All they needed to do was make a dress and mittens from pieces of jute and old rags. The two women labored all night and in the gray of the dawn set off for the plantation.

It was harvesttime.

The sun was still hiding coyly in a corner of the sky. Yet already dozens of men and women in rags were busy working. The carts drawn by oxen drained of their force trundled through the cane pieces. Not anyone can be a cane bundler. The job is carried out by federations, genuine convoys of olden times, made up of elderly women, even very old women, who are too worn out for weeding and clearing.

Did José the foreman, a mulatto himself, take pity on Victoire's belly?

Whatever the case, he accepted her request, and under a sun growing bolder by the minute, she braved exhaustion, the sting of the cane, and dizziness in order to deliver her bundles of sugarcane.

It was Lourdes who was so happy! Hoisting up her skirt over her bow legs the color of *kako dou,* she indulged in so much tomfoolery that she managed to get a smile out of Victoire.

Coming after so many bad days, the evening was blissful. And the following night even more blissful.

Alas! The following morning, no sooner had they set foot in the field than a song rose up amid the laughter and vulgar jibes. It was about a mulatto girl, a slut fallen on hard times, who, after having had her fill of men, stole the bread out of the mouths of her poor black neighbors. Victoire took to her heels and fled.

This was the first and last experience my grandmother had of the cane fields.

Even so, she never gave up. Despite the condition of her rounding belly, she was constantly looking for work. Shortly afterward, her real life began. I next find her as a cook in the service of Rochelle Dulieu-Beaufort, the wife of the owner of the sugar factory at Pirogue. Cook! Let us confess it was a bold claim, since at the Jovials, we may recall, all she ever did was help Danila. Yet from the very first day her destiny took shape. She proved to have an incomparable gift. She won over the Dulieu-Beaufort family with a cream of pumpkin and black crab soup. The Dulieu-Beauforts symbolized the reversal of fortune undergone by certain white Creoles. They had in turn grown tobacco and indigo and set up a coffee plantation, which, according to them, produced the best coffee in Guadeloupe. One of their relatives, a friend of Dominique Guesde who, like him, was a dilettante writer, had invented the slogan:

Sèl kafé di kalité, sé kafé Gwadloup. (The only quality coffee is coffee from Guadeloupe.)

Alas, in the wake of a hurricane, Marie-Galante lost all its coffee and cotton plants. The family had now turned to sugar while in La Pointe Monsieur Souques was preparing to nose out all the factory owners with his Darboussier plant. They were thus living sparingly at Maule. In their elegant house made of solid wood with a roof of wooden tiles, Rochelle rationed the oil and rice for meals and lit only one paraffin lamp to light twelve rooms. Victoire was unable to present any references and what's more was pregnant. No problem! Two excellent reasons to underpay her!

The Dulieu-Beauforts had managed to engage their eldest daughter, Anne-Marie, a sixteen-year-old beauty, to Boniface Walberg, whose ups and downs in the sugar industry had prompted him to become a trader on the quai Lardenoy in La Pointe. Outraged at being sold to a man she despised for his lack of musical education, Anne-Marie locked herself in her room with her viola and played and played.

Strange, this passion for music in a materialist family! A loving godmother, on noticing her unusual ear for music, had given her a violin on her fourth birthday. She slept with it tight between her legs. It was the first thing she grabbed hold of on wakening. She had forced her parents to send her to the conservatoire in Boulogne, near Paris. Besides the violin, she was learning to play the guitar and the recorder when the family ruin obliged her to return to Marie-Galante. Ever since, she had made a good job of making herself loathsome to everyone.

Anne-Marie didn't take long noticing the new cook. Not because she could rustle up a sublime gumbo, a creamy concoction obtained by adding additional okra leaves, but because twice she had entered her room unexpectedly and surprised Victoire, holding her viola to her shoulder.

"Do you like my music?" she had asked, surprised.

"Oui, mamzel," Victoire had whispered.

Do the blacks have an ear for things other than the *bamboula*? If yes, this would back up Anne-Marie's theory that there should be no hierarchy between different types of music. Those who called the *gwo ka*, *bèlè*, merengue, or *mazouk* a lot of *bamboula*, in other words primitive music, exasperated her. Their rhythms were different from a sonata or a symphony, that's all. However, she hadn't had time to verify the exactitude of her audacious point of view since Victoire, pushing in front of her a belly that now could not be ignored, had run out.

Thus was born a solid, mysterious relationship that must have exasperated and set quite a number of people talking. It was only to end with the death of Victoire, called to God long before Anne-Marie, who ended her life obese and ninety years old. But we will come back to that.

FIVE

My mother was born on April 28, 1890, at four o'clock in the morning.

Victoire christened her Jeanne Marie Marthe. I have no idea what motivated her choice of this string of first names.

When she went into labor the evening before, Dodose Quidal, the midwife, looked in and then left, predicting the child would not come into this world just then. She proved to be right. The next time Dodose pushed open the door of her cabin, Victoire was expulsing her daughter in a flow of blood and fecal matter. We know that any birth is a butchery. The child weighed six and a half pounds. As soon as she emerged from her mother's womb, she was beautiful, my mother. A skin as soft as a sapodilla, a mass of hair more curly than frizzy or downright kinky, at least to begin with, for things were to change when she was seven or eight, a perfectly oval face, a high forehead, sparkling almond-shaped eyes, prominent cheekbones, and a well-defined mouth. She was the spitting image of her father. Once Dodose had wiped her with a cloth, she laid her on her mother's chest, where the baby greedily guzzled on a breast. It was then that Victoire burst into tears. For the very first time.

She hadn't cried when Caldonia died.

She hadn't cried when Dernier ran away. I use this verb, "ran," although we will never know for certain whether Dernier ever knew about her pregnancy.

She hadn't cried when the Jovials threw her out like a slut.

She hadn't cried when Thérèse left for France barricaded in bitterness and hatred.

Was it then, through her tears, that she swore to her daughter she would watch over her and give her every possible chance in life so that nobody would ever trample on her daughter like they had trampled on her? Education, education, swear to God, would be her emancipation. Her daughter would be educated. She would sacrifice herself for that.

Dodose expressed amazement when she received the placenta in her hands. Piecemeal. Stained in red. Greenish in places. Foul-smelling. It boded no good. In fact, three hours later Victoire came down with a high fever. Dr. Nesty, a mulatto who had studied in Paris, called to the rescue, confirmed it was caused by an infection of the placenta. For days on end, despite leeches to draw out the bad blood and lemon hip baths, Victoire struggled between life and death. She was covered in sweat. She pushed aside Lourdes, who never stopped sobbing. She was delirious, calling for Caldonia and Eliette, her mother whom she had never known. Day in and day out the Dulieu-Beauforts' carriage trundled along the clayey, never stony, tracks of Marie-Galante. A tearful Anne-Marie begged her mother not to abandon her poor cook. Mme. Dulieu-Beaufort, always at the disposition of charity, obeyed the word of God, who was speaking through her daughter. At her request, the priest at Saint-Louis came to confess Victoire and give her communion. Was it the effect of these last sacraments?

To everyone's surprise, Victoire recovered.

On the eighteenth day of her illness, sitting next to her on the mattress of her *kabann*, Dr. Nesty took her hand, reassuring her she would live, but whispering that now that she was sixteen she would never see her blood again or have any more children. I think I can guess what Victoire felt. In our societies, even today, to be a mother is the only true vocation of a woman. Sterility means nothing less than dragging around a useless body, deprived of its essential virtue. Papaya tree that bears no papayas. Mango tree that gives no mangoes. Cucumber without seeds. A hollow husk.

Victoire's pain and disappointment no doubt surged back toward her heart, which became a burning niche for Jeanne, the daughter whom the Good Lord in His mysterious ways decided would be the one and only. She never managed, however, to translate into acts the devouring passion she felt for her beautiful baby. None of those cannibal caresses like those of certain mothers who eat up their children with kisses. None of those absurd pet names. None of those intimate little games. Constantly busying herself around her baby, she remained silent as if shackled from inside. Her hands darted around with sharp, precise gestures, as cutting as machetes.

There were moments of gentleness even so.

She would make Jeanne delicious little dishes and was overjoyed at her appetite. When Jeanne wriggled and whimpered like any child trying to get to sleep, she would take the music box, turn the handle, and softly sing along while the little girl was lulled to sleep with the song from *Carmen*:

L'amour est un oiseau rebelle

THERE REMAINED, HOWEVER, one final station of her calvary.

These were incredible times. So that there should be no mistake, the priests baptized on Sundays those infants born into the holy sacrament of marriage who slept blissfully in fine lace blouses. On Saturdays, it was the turn of the infants born in sin. These represented 95 percent of all the births. On Saturdays, lines of newborns, some of them choking from the heat, wailing in the arms of their godmothers, stretched as far as the street. But Saturday could not be the day for Victoire. Her sin was neither venal nor mortal. It was extraordinary. Her daughter was Satan in person. Father Amallyas, the priest at Grand Bourg, was a friend of Gaëtane's and her confessor: purely for form's sake, since the good soul had nothing on her conscience, except perhaps her liking for curaçao from Holland. He was also a friend of the mayor's. He would stuff himself at Sunday lunch at the Jovials and turn a deaf ear to Fulgence's speeches inspired by Voltaire. He thus refused to baptize Jeanne and in a confidential note dated May 10, 1890, he urged the priests at Saint-Louis and Capesterre to do the same.

Such unchristian behavior offended Rochelle Dulieu-Beaufort. How could a priest condemn an innocent child to eternal damnation? She turned once again to her friend the priest at Saint-Louis and begged him to ignore this shameful directive. Jeanne, dressed in a gauze robe and wearing a bonnet worn by the last of the Dulieu-Beauforts' ten children, was baptized in the chapel at Maule. Anne-Marie and her younger brother Etienne acted as godmother and godfather.

There were no guests, not even Lourdes. No *chodo* custard, no cake. A drop of aniseed-flavored lemonade. With a pound of flour from France, Victoire made fritters and waffles. After the ceremony was over Anne-Marie, for once all smiles, improvised on her viola *Souvenir des Antilles,* a selection of Creole melodies composed by M. Gottschalk, the well-known pianist who, the previous year, had won fame during his tour of Martinique and Guadeloupe.

Such an act of cruelty aimed at her child was probably the last straw. It prompted Victoire to make a major decision: leave La Treille and Marie-Galante.

It is likely that Anne-Marie also gave her the idea, since she had moved to La Pointe following her marriage. Without her, under Rochelle Dulieu-Beaufort's iron rule, Maule and Marie-Galante were nothing better than a prison.

Informed of the plan, Lourdes clapped her hands and offered to accompany Victoire. Oh yes! Leave! What had they to lose? A ramshackle cabin. Marie-Galante was going from bad to worse. We could even say she was dying. There was less and less work. The sugar factories were in decline. Let's take Elie as an example. Exile had made him into a success story. Turning his back on the whims of fishing, he had found a job in a factory at Goyave specializing in the processing of ramie. There was only one point on which aunt and niece were in disagreement: Lourdes insisted on doing the rounds at La Treille to present her farewells. To go off in secret, without saying a word, would be nothing other than self-mutilation. Some of the inhabitants remembered her mother, Caldonia, and had witnessed her birth, tenth in line. Some had attended her christening. Others her first communion. Consequently, she would appropriate their memories in order to alleviate her uprooting. Victoire fiercely refused to hear of such a proposition. Never, never would she step into the homes of people who had humiliated her and hated her ever since she was a little girl. She could never forget their sarcastic remarks and the names of Ti-Sapoti and Volan they gave her. When she was lying sick at death's door, how many of them had troubled to pay her a visit, say a prayer or a Hail Mary?

The only person she visited to explain why she was leaving was Rochelle Dulieu-Beaufort. It was then that Rochelle's mean and cantankerous character got the upper hand and she heaped insults on her.

"What! Who will cook for me now?"

So that was how Victoire rewarded her for all the kindness she had shown her and her bastard child? She was truly a wretch, a dreg from hell who was hated by everyone on Marie-Galante.

I CAN SEE them on that morning of June 1890 as they leave their native land.

Victoire has wrapped Jeanne in a white baby's cape and is hugging her close. The infant, who is hot under all this wool, is constantly fidgeting. She manages to wriggle free and pokes out her head, observing her surroundings with curiosity.

People on the jetty are guessing the weight of the wicker basket that Lourdes is carrying. Are they leaving for good, these shameless hussies, these *dames-gabrielle*? Let them take their loose living elsewhere so that young girls from good families can marry at church with veil and crown!

With not enough money for the steamship that leaves Grand Bourg every Wednesday for La Pointe, the trio settles down at the front of the schooner *Arc-en-Ciel*. The stern is reserved for merchandise, animals, piglets, chickens, and goats. Rocked by the breeze and the movement of the waves, Jeanne soon falls asleep. Lourdes bites into a *danikite* doughnut.

What was Victoire thinking during the never-ending crossing? Did she realize she was seeing Marie-Galante for the very last time? The odds are that she was oblivious to the splendid panorama: the islands of Les Saintes playing dice on the velvet of the ocean, the colored ridges of the Soufrière volcano, and the gauzelike scarves of clouds. Her only thoughts were for Caldonia and the days spent with her. Did she regret turning her back on this flat island where lay the graves of her mother and grandmother?

As a precaution against seasickness she had brought along some lemons. Her tense fist became sticky from squeezing the slices as she unconsciously forgot to put them in her mouth.

Since the wind was brisk, they arrived early midafternoon at the entrance to the harbor at La Pointe through a difficult narrow passage where the isles of Cochon, Pitre, and Montroux drift toward the headland at Jarry. At that time, one side of the Place de la Victoire, devoid of wharfs, came to rest on a quiet beach while the other three sides were lined by the trees of liberty, the sandbox trees planted by M. Victor Hughes. In the neighboring streets, cases and bundles of merchandise were piled up in front of the stores amid heaps of packing straw and canvas. True to their habits, a crowd of loudmouthed and ragged dockers stared at the young girls. Lourdes was offended by the catcalls and lewd invitations, whereas Victoire kept walking, head lowered, hugging her child to her heart.

Once again they didn't have enough money to pay for the coach that traveled from La Pointe to Goyave in two hours and forty-five minutes. They had to make do with one of the sailboats that linked up with Petit Bourg by way of the Petit Cul-de-Sac. Since they were to set sail at dawn, they had to sleep at the house of a certain Sigismonde Quidal on the road to Les Abymes, who asked next to nothing for the room and pig-foot soup.

They left at four in the morning, the baby muffled up to her eyes, the adults shivering in the cool of the predawn. They had been kept awake by the chimes of the church of Saint-Pierre and Saint-Paul. They had just dropped off when the din of the night soil carts and the smell of their contents abundantly spread over the sidewalks once again interrupted their sleep. At La Pointe, the town's sanitation services resembled Rio de Janeiro's, a city that didn't have cesspools either. Excrement was poured into barrels, the contents of which were then thrown into the sea.

On the other side of the bay, nestled up against the mountains, the busy streets of Petit Bourg hinted at the crowded town it is today. Lourdes and Victoire did not linger and set off for Goyave, carrying the baby in turns as they walked the six or seven kilometers. Victoire was frightened by the roar of the rivers and gullies that wound under the rope bridges, as well as by the stifling thickness of the vigorous vegetation ready to swallow her up: all types of trees whose armpits were eaten away by wild pineapples, creepers, orchids, tree ferns, and shrubs. This landscape was so different from the flat cane fields of Marie-Galante, dotted here and there by windmills. At times they were forced into the ditch to avoid the oxcarts, trundling along amid the cracking of whips, the swearing of the drivers, and the creaking of the axles.

The town of Goyave was nothing more than a hamlet. A few cabins scattered along the seashore. But it took them hours to find Elie's. Fortunately, at the church that had been totally destroyed by the 1843 earthquake and rebuilt in stone, the asthmatic priest was kind enough to give them directions. They had to walk along the railroad tracks, used for transporting the cane to the Marquisat factory in Capesterre, until they reached the entrance to the beach at Sainte-Claire. Dusk was falling when they finally knocked on the right door.

Alas! Bobette was giving birth to her twelfth child.

You would have expected it to be a mere formality, to go off without a hitch, as the saying goes. Far from it. The poor woman was losing pints of blood and screaming like an animal in agony. Some matronly neighbors were busy carrying scarlet-stained sheets and calabashes of water. The following morning Elie was a widower, father of Eliacin, the fifth son, a pale crybaby of a boy who never got over the death of his mother. Elie suffered a lot. In his own reserved way, he had adored his Bobette. It's true she was no longer very lovely. It's true she had become fat, enormous even, from giving birth, and from eating breadfruit, *dombwé* dumplings, and thick soup. Even so, she had meant a lot to him.

The next morning, they were getting ready for the wake ceremony when a tilbury jolted into the sunken lane. A young woman got out. Blonde, perfumed, dressed like a princess out of a fairy tale, it was Anne-Marie Walberg. You can imagine the effect this visit had on the wretched surroundings. People gaped in embarrassment.

It is obvious that Anne-Marie and Victoire, who were at an age for conspiring and scheming in secret, had agreed to meet up at Goyave. The former had assured the latter that, newly wedded to a man of prominence, she was in a position to help her. There remained, however, a number of questions concerning this shocking behavior. Out of respect for her uncle's mourning, couldn't Victoire have postponed her plans? No way. The two accomplices did their whispering on the doorstep. Then Anne-Marie went and kneeled at the side of the deceased, laid out on her bed, and squeezed into her best dress. In the meantime, Victoire gathered up her old clothes and cradled Jeanne in her arms. At first nobody could understand what was going on. Their eyes were opened when both women climbed into the tilbury. The concert of "Oh, Good Lord!" alerted Lourdes, who came out with the foreboding of misfortune. On seeing her, Victoire sat the child on her lap and made her wave with one of her tiny hands.

That was how Jeanne said farewell to her origins of Marie-Galante.

She was never to return to her native island. She was never to know any member of her mother's family. Her mother never described to her La Treille or Grand Bourg and she never spoke to us, her children, about it. Is that why Marie-Galante in my imagination signifies a mythical land, a lost paradise waiting to be repossessed? I had lost my placenta there, buried under a tree I could no longer find. Elie was often tempted to force his way into the Walbergs' home. But feelings about distance were different then. La Pointe, which is situated at a mere twenty or so kilometers from Goyave, seemed to be on the other side of the world. Elie got the impression it could only be reached after a voyage as long and perilous as that taken by Christopher Columbus's caravels, the *Niña* and the *Pinta*.

He renounced such an undertaking. I know that later on one of his sons managed to draw closer to Jeanne. Occasionally, he would turn up at mealtimes. He was the only one who forced open the barriers erected by our family.

MORE THAN TWENTY years after the event, Lourdes, who had settled down in Goyave, married a fisherman and produced ten children, still lamented:

"Victoire, she was my little sister. *Sésé an mwen*. Her child, she was my child. *Ti moun an mwen*. It's as if she came out of my womb. When she turned her back on us like that, I wanted to die. And then I understood. What she wanted for her child was an upstairs-downstairs house made of concrete and wood. Behind it, a hurricane shelter. In the bedroom, a four-poster bed and a stool to climb up into it. That's what she wanted and that's what she got. But you don't trample on the hearts of one's family for all that nonsense. Just for that. It might be all right to insult the living. But you should never disrespect the dead! Can you imagine! Bobette was lying on the other side of the wall. Victoire left without even kneeling to whisper a good-bye. I'll say it again, you don't disrespect the dead. Otherwise they take their revenge and their revenge is terrible. You can't escape it, even if you run in every direction like a rat smoked out from a cane field. That's why, I'm pretty sure, she never knew a single day of happiness. You can't have a wicked heart and be happy."

Elie was more temperate, even though Victoire's behavior had sickened him, he whose feelings had already been so hurt. On that day he had lost not only his wife, but through Victoire and Jeanne all that remained of his beloved twin sister, Eliette. Stoical, he shook his head:

"Life is an Arab stallion. It throws us to the ground one after the other. If the cane doesn't kill you, something else will. Wicked heart? No, I don't think Victoire had a wicked heart. She simply was looking for a better life for her child and that's what we all want. Isn't that right?"

In this discussion I will try and excuse Victoire. Anne-Marie promised to come to her aid by procuring her a job as a cook. Not only was it a way of rescuing her, but also of ensuring a roof for her child. But Anne-Marie had no use for Victoire's ragtag relations of field Negroes, country bookies, and boo-boos. She didn't want them on her floor. Victoire, who was in no position to protest, had to accept her conditions. I have to admit too that Caldonia's death, Dernier's desertion, and all the vile deeds of Marie-Galante had hardened her heart. She had loved her grandmother so much that, deprived of her warmth, she withdrew into herself. As for the island that had treated her so badly, she returned the compliment.

AROUND 1892 La Pointe, "the yellow city," numbered a little under twenty thousand souls. Prosperous in spite of her incredible filth, she had been the prime victim of natural catastrophes. We may recall that after the February 1843 earthquake, rear admiral Gourbeyre, then governor of Guadeloupe, addressed the following dramatic message to his ministry in charge: "At the moment I am writing to you I have learned that La Pointe no longer exists."

He was mistaken; La Pointe was born again like a phoenix from its ashes. But it was still not out of the woods. In September 1865 a powerful hurricane devastated it once again. Six years later a fire destroyed it entirely. As a consequence Boniface Walberg, heir in 1889 to his uncle Ludovic, who had returned to France given the difficulties of the sugar industry, reinforced with masonry the house on the rue de Nassau, a little outside the center on the western outskirts of town. He even went so far as to cast a concrete slab on the roof, which had the annoying habit of flying off at the slightest blow of wind, and then cover it with slate tiles. His house was now a replica of his store, whose facade stretched twenty meters along the quai Lardenoy, adjacent to the businessmen's club where they held the most magnificent of balls. The house on the rue Nassau had one particular feature: a secret garden at the back, hidden from prying eyes, like certain houses in London. Behind the kitchen and the washhouse there were almost a thousand meters of lawn where a large-leafed licuala and two blue palm trees grew. Anastasie, Uncle Ludovic's wife, had planted some pomegranate trees with bright red flowers.

We note that the name of Boniface Walberg was listed in the *General Business Almanac*, which included the names of the most important merchants. His employees, whom he treated with a rare correctness at a time of inequality, had invented the half-affectionate, half-mocking nickname of *Bèf pòtoriko* because he was short-legged, thickset, with a forehead hidden under a fringe of hair as black as the coat of a bull from Puerto Rico. They credited him also with a member that would not have been out of place on such a creature. If you believed the gossip, the *dames-gabrielle* from a bordello on the Morne à Cayes, which he frequented regularly before his affair with Victoire, avoided him, fearful of his iron rod. Underneath this appearance he was in fact someone unsure of himself, timorous, even fainthearted. He had let himself be hoodwinked into marrying Anne-Marie Dulieu-Beaufort, who had brought him as a dowry nothing more than a violin, not even a Stradivarius, a mundane instrument purchased for a few francs at an instrument maker's in La Pointe. Authoritarian, and a head taller than he, she intimidated him to such a degree that he made love to her only on the fifth night of their marriage. It had been a fiasco. Ever since, he had been such a rare visitor to her bed that when in exasperation she announced she was pregnant, he was close to thinking it was another machination of the Holy Ghost.

He started eating dinner alone, having learned that his wife had gone to Goyave without telling him, as usual.

"Goyave? What on earth is she doing in Goyave?"

Flaminia, the servant, had no idea.

Those who know their geography know that the river Salée is the name of the stretch of sea that separates Grande Terre and La Pointe from Basse-Terre and Goyave. A barge operated as a ferry to cross it. Anne-Marie and Victoire had to wait their turn for two full hours, stuck between numerous carriages.

When they arrived at rue de Nassau it was already dark.

Holding his spoon midair, Boniface looked at the strange trio that came into view. Anne-Marie, regal, wearing a low-cut dress revealing the cameo jewel nestled against her ample breasts; a small, frail mulatto girl wearing a black-and-white-check madras headtie whose pale eyes were boring into him; and a chubby baby who was exhausted by the trip, going by her shrieks.

"This is Victoire, our new cook." Anne-Marie made the introductions with an air of authority.

Oh, Boniface said to himself, befuddled by Victoire's gaze, *so we needed a new cook. Flaminia wasn't enough.*

"À vòt sèvis, mèt!" the mulatto girl murmured in Creole, in a voice that, like her gaze, sent shivers down his spine.

Before he had had time to emit the sound of an answer or pronounce a banal *"ka ou fè"* greeting, the trio had left the room and swept up the stairs.

Flaminia reappeared carrying the cod *brandade* and red beans.

"She's putting her in the Regency room," she hissed.

She hated Anne-Marie, whose spitefulness outdid her own. In her youth, she had brought Boniface up during his childhood on Marie-Galante, been one of his father's mistresses, and kept house for him while he was a bachelor. For him, she had left the scents of her island for this filthy town that stank of excrement and dead dogs and where the *dames-gabrielle* shamelessly traded their charms.

The room they half jokingly called the Regency room, the loveliest in the house, was situated on the third floor. It owed its name to two Regency-style armchairs with lion's feet and a sofa in the same style, mounted likewise on lion's claws, which served as a bed.

More than anyone, Boniface dreaded Anne-Marie's moods and stinging repartee. He kept mum about the extravagant idea of attributing the Regency room to a cook and her brat, thus deserving once more the pet name Flaminia had given to him, Pontius Pilate.

Disgusted, Flaminia showered him with a look of commiseration.

SIX

Officially, then, Victoire was hired as a cook in the service of the Walbergs. Yet there is no document to confirm this. With her very first meal she astounded the entire family. Far from merely cooking Creole dishes with panache, she used her imagination to invent them. On her second day, she served up a guinea fowl *au gros sel* and two types of cabbage that sent Boniface, who, we must confess, was already under her charm, into raptures.

What I am claiming is the legacy of this woman, who apparently did not leave any. I want to establish the link between her creativity and mine, to switch from the savors, the colors, and the smells of meat and vegetables to those of words. Victoire did not have a name for her dishes and that didn't seem to bother her. Most of her days she spent locked up in the temple of her kitchen, a small shack behind the house, set slightly back from the washhouse. Not saying a word, head bent, absorbed over her kitchen range like a writer hunched over her computer. She would let nobody chop a chive or press a lemon, as if in the kitchen no task was humble enough when aiming at perfection. She frequently tasted the food, but once the composition was completed, she never touched it again.

Her reputation for the time being, however, remained within

the boundaries of the rue de Nassau. Since neither Anne-Marie nor Boniface entertained at home, folk in La Pointe for a long time knew nothing of the jewel they possessed.

In the meantime, they settled into a ménage of three, even four, whispered malicious gossip, though we have no proof. Contrary to the usual practice of women of her class, who often led a life of leisure, Anne-Marie privileged music over writing and did not keep a diary. All we know of her is through a regular correspondence of no great interest, comprised of letters to her mother, Rochelle, and to her brothers and sisters, especially Etienne, who was her favorite. We can only go by a number of clues. The servants' gossip, led by Flaminia, and the spitefulness of the white Creoles in La Pointe, all were in agreement that the true Madame Walberg was not who we thought she was. Unlike most children, Jeanne was weaned very early on and placed in a box room that had been converted into an English nursery for the Walberg children while under the supervision of a *mabo*. The furniture in the Regency room was changed. The sofa, elegant but uncomfortable, especially for two people, was replaced by a sleigh bed. As soon as they repealed the Edict of March 1724, which had been lying around for over a hundred years in the drawers of the Ministry for the Colonies, prohibiting a donation inter vivos to any descendant of slaves, Boniface transferred a sum to the account of Jeanne, which she drew out on reaching her majority. Later on he included her in his will. A letter that Anne-Marie wrote to Etienne, quoted in a history thesis defended at the College for Social Sciences in Paris, contains the following sentence, which is open to interpretation:

"I loathe the life I lead, even though our faithful and beloved Victoire consoles me by relieving me of many an obligation."

In the same thesis, entitled "From Plantation Owner to Businessman: A History of the White Creoles in Guadeloupe," my attention was also caught by a letter that Boniface wrote to Evremond, his older brother, who was very close to him, although they went different ways: "My life would be filled with unhappiness if it weren't constantly illuminated by the devotion of my faithful Victoire."

We note that each time reference is made to the word "faithful." We might very well ask ourselves to whom Victoire was faithful. Was it to Anne-Marie? To Boniface? Or was she pursuing her own private ambition that centered on Jeanne? Only Jeanne?

Let us add that in the Antilles there is a time-honored practice where the white male marries the white female, but takes his pleasure with every mulatto or black girl he can lay his hands on. Slavery or no slavery.

As for imagining an intimate relationship between Anne-Marie and Victoire, I refuse to believe it. If some people have no trouble going there, it is because the tradition of both masculine and feminine homosexuality is well established in the Antilles. There is abundant research to prove that the masters entered into such passionate and stifling relations with their domestic slaves that most of the latter preferred to work in the fields rather than in the house. At the end of the nineteenth century female homosexuality was still thriving. In La Pointe the *zanmis* were very open about their relations, living together, sporting the same costumes and dancing lasciviously during carnival. One of them by the name of Zéna composed a beguine for her beloved, which got the whole island dancing:

> *Ninon, mwen renmé vou*
> *A la foli danmou*
> *Ninon, mwen renmé vou*
> *Kon foufou renmé miyel*
> *E kon bouch renmé bô*

When her beloved left her for another she lamented:

> *Aïe, aïe, aïe, mwen vlé mò*
> *Pa ni soleye ankò*
> *La vi pa dous*
> *Mwen vlé mò*

I PREFER TO believe that Anne-Marie and Victoire fell head over heels into an exceptional friendship at first sight and remained accomplices to the very end.

Was Victoire rewarded for her services?

Mulatto women one generation before hers had no scruples fleecing their white lovers and mocking taboos. When they were forbidden to wear shoes they decorated their toes with diamonds given them by the very same lovers. It was obvious that Victoire had lost such a gift. Apparently she never had a penny to her name. When she thought it absolutely necessary, Anne-Marie had a shapeless *golle* dress made for her and bought her a headtie or a pair of shoes. Always the same model: embroidered velvet slippers. On the other hand, Anne-Marie devoted herself entirely to the care of Jeanne, who was always rigged out like a duchess, which later on entitled Anne-Marie to consider herself unfairly treated as a benefactress.

Whatever the nature of the ties that bonded them together, Victoire and Anne-Marie wore their social status outwardly: Anne-Marie authoritarian and brusque, Victoire silent and constantly in the background. The servants on the rue de Nassau, however, in their terror put them both in the same basket and declared that Victoire was the worse of the two:

"Victwa, sé pli môvé-la."

Likewise, throughout La Pointe the silhouette of Victoire trotting behind her haughty mistress, who was a head taller than she was, soon came to be loathed. The white Creoles thought she should be mistrusted like all mulatto women, "the women of no shame," as they were called. It was said that they had always dreamed of "taking their revenge on their masters with the arms of pleasure," according to the expression of the priest at Emberménil, Father Grégoire. As for the people of color, meaning mulattos, who were increasingly numerous, they took offense at the condition of one of their own. Slavery was over. To prostitute yourself for your master was a shame. Only the Negroes, too busy struggling for social ascension or survival, took no interest in Victoire.

Both women's lives seemed to be dominated by the same passion: God and music. Up till then, God, who had not worked any miracles for Victoire, did not mean much to her. It was on contact with Anne-Marie that she became religious. At least in her deeds.

Every morning she would walk up the rue de Nassau to the rue Barbès, cross the Place de la Liberté, and climb up the steps of Saint-Pierre and Saint-Paul to attend five o'clock mass, the so-called dawn mass. Like the rest of La Pointe, this church was evidence of God's power. One hundred and fifty years earlier it had been razed to the ground by Victor Hughes. Then an earthquake had destroyed it and it had been damaged by fire and a hurricane. Each time, it had risen from its ruins.

As I have already said, Victoire clearly signified in her comportment that she was the subaltern. She followed Anne-Marie to the altar, three steps behind, and took communion after her. When Anne-Marie came out of Father Rouard's confessional, Victoire would go in and kneel down. Yet they were both given the same three dozen rosaries. Such a light penitence! They surely hadn't confessed they shared the same man and perhaps, at times, took pleasure in each other. Confessions are only made to institutionalize the lies.

Sunday was the day for high mass.

Thursday for Anne-Marie, a member of the Congregation of the Sacred Heart of Jesus, was the day for calalu and rice. La Pointe at that time counted a considerable number of needy, the poor *maléré* as they were called. In fact, there were two distinct towns. The town of the well-to-do white Creoles and a few mulattoes, residing around the cathedral, and the town of the *maléré*, the Negroes cast out to the edges of the Vatable Canal district. Dug by a former governor in an attempt to drain the surrounding marshland, the canal had soon become a dumping ground. The traveler Toussaint Chantrans wrote in 1883: "The banks of the canal are nothing but foul mud where rubbish of all sorts rots and spreads a nauseating stench."

The *maléré* took only one meal a day consisting of root vegetables moistened with a little oil, together with microscopic pieces of beef, salt pork, or codfish for the luckier ones. With an apron tied around her waist, blonde like one of the Good Lord's angels, Anne-Marie, assisted by Victoire, piously served the long lines of ragged individuals in front of the trestle tables set up on the sidewalk. On receiving their plateful, the *maléré* thanked profoundly their benefactress for the goodness of her heart before casting a malevolent gaze at Victoire.

I have often asked myself the reason for this animosity. I think I now know why. Given her status as a servant, Victoire did not possess the aura of holiness that haloed the white master. Her presence was disturbing and humiliating.

APART FROM THAT, they never missed vespers or rosary, Tenebrae or the month of Mary. In short, none of those many ceremonies that the Catholic Church contrives to devise for the greater happiness of its followers. At carnival, however, when the devil appears as a *moko* zombie dancing on stilts, ringing bells, and asking for coins, they would close doors and windows.

I don't blame Anne-Marie the same way I blamed Thérèse Jovial for having neglected to educate Victoire because Anne-Marie taught her music. For her it was the supreme form of expression. Ever since Boniface had started snoring in the very middle of Mendelssohn's Concerto for Violin and a great many guests had dozed off at the same moment, Anne-Marie had taken this as a pretext not to perform in public.

"It's like casting pearls before swine," she would say.

Every afternoon she would lock herself in her room with Victoire. She taught her the rudiments of the guitar—a few simple chords over which my grandmother spread her childlike hands—as well as the recorder. But Victoire preferred to listen to Anne-Marie. They were usually personal compositions that she labored over, sending Délia to buy her pens, ink, and lined paper from the Simon Matureau store on the rue de la Liberté, now rue Alexandre Isaac.

Apparently she composed beguines, rhythms that were becoming wildly popular in Guadeloupe as well as Martinique. I regret that these pieces have disappeared entirely. Thus, we shall never know whether Anne-Marie was a genius or merely a good musician.

I can but imagine the emotions that inspired this strange pair in the heat of the afternoon as the town of La Pointe lay in its siesta under mosquito nets. They were in ecstasy under the torrent of trills and arpeggios. Anne-Marie, standing, frenziedly stroking her bow. Victoire seated in a rocking chair, cradling the guitar, humming in her reedy voice or dreaming silently like Gauguin's *Brooding Woman*. As refreshment, they would drink aniseed-flavored lemonade.

Like every lady of her station, Anne-Marie hardly set foot out of doors. Utterly drained after these sessions, she would sit in the back garden or on her balcony. She would watch the day as it drew to a close, the sky turning orange over the harbor and the darkening silhouette of the ring of hills. The stench that wafted up from the outlying districts upset her. In the meantime, Victoire had gone back down to the kitchen to prepare supper, only a tad more frugal than lunch. She then concocted some pâtés that she seasoned with rat poison and laid down on the sidewalk for the stray dogs. These dogs were the bane of La Pointe, running by day in aggressive, mangy packs. It was not unusual for them to attack small children. At night their yelping and dog fights made it impossible to sleep. To poison them was the only way to get rid of them, since the municipality did absolutely nothing. In the morning their stiffened corpses with bloodied muzzles piled up in the garbage carts that crisscrossed the town.

One picture haunts Jeanne's memory: that of her mother impassively preparing these macabre meals with the same hands that prepared feasts for the living. Initiated into Greek and Roman mythology, the child thought she was seeing one of those Fates who presided in turn with equal impartiality over the birth and death of humans.

As you can see, life at the Walbergs was fairly monotonous. I wonder whether such monotony was not often burdensome, whether Victoire was not often tempted to slam the door and go back to her own people, their pleasures, and their exuberant, violent forms of entertainment.

The opulent upstairs-downstairs houses or those with yard and garden on the rue de Nassau soon petered out and gave way to the Vatable Canal district. Although by day it was neither lovely to look at nor cheerful to behold, this all changed in the evening. The district became a fairylike realm of sleazy dives and rum shops aglow with alcohol amid the din of dominoes and rough shouts. The dances began early Saturday and the shameless *bòbòs* would lift their petticoats over their velvet thighs as they danced the *roulé*, *gragé*, *mendé*, and *lewoz*.

But this class to which she belonged had rejected her from early childhood. Because of her color. This color, without money or, failing that, without education, is nothing but a curse. Once she pushed open the door of one of these dives, a niggerman would be bound to mount her like a *tambouyé*, his drum. Afterward he would turn his back on her like Dernier did.

We learn, thanks to *L'Echo pointois*, that sometime in November 1890 Victoire accompanied Anne-Marie to a concert in the Bobineau Hall, rue Barbès. *L'Echo pontois* had replaced *L'Illustration*, dead and buried, and likewise claimed to represent polite society. Anne-Marie wanted both of them to hear Léo Delibes' *Lakmé* interpreted by the Capitole troupe from Toulouse. This story of a young Indian girl and an English officer sounded interesting. Anne-Marie's presence that evening caused a sensation. She was eight months pregnant and at that stage it was indecent to be seen in public. People wondered where her husband was and considered it out of place for her to attend a social evening alone with a servant.

We do not know what Victoire thought of the concert. But we do know that Anne-Marie was disappointed. She complained in a letter to her beloved Etienne that the acoustics were bad and in the tenth row where she was seated she could hardly hear a thing. The opera itself did not appeal to her. As for that melody which had been given such a glowing tribute in the *Courrier mélomane*, commonly called the Bell Song—"Where is the young Hindu girl going"—she declared it highly overrated.

WE DO NOT know for certain what Victoire's feelings were, sharing her bed with *Bèf pòtoriko*.

Everything leads us to believe that she first obeyed Anne-Marie and agreed to relieve her of a loathsome conjugal duty. Yet gradually she grew attached to Boniface and in my opinion ended up loving him. Proof of this was her grief when he died.

Boniface was not devoid of a sort of coy charm. He had, therefore, always been his mother's favorite, taking precedence over his more handsome brothers. I have to say in all truth that most people thought it was simply a calculation on Victoire's part. She saw in him nothing but a rich "stepfather" for her daughter.

Let us dream a little.

Was Victoire sensual? Was she fond of lovemaking? Everything points to the affirmative.

Nevertheless, men at that time bothered little about women's pleasure. Women themselves seldom expected to reach a climax. Boniface thrust himself into Victoire four to five times a night. She had an orgasm somewhat by chance. Afterward, they slept in each other's arms, united by a fear of the dark, a survival of their childhood. When it rained or the wind blew, they felt especially close. The sleigh bed rolled like a sailboat on a swell of blackness. Boniface clutched Victoire against his heart as they waited with bated breath and open eyes for a break in the weather. At the end of the nineteenth century, earthquakes were a common occurrence. For no reason whatsoever, a muffled groan would rise up from the depths. The wooden house would vibrate and crack in all its joints. Objects would fall to the ground. Pictures would fall off the wall. Then everything returned to normal. It was more frightening than anything else, and night resumed its unwavering march.

At four in the morning, the first up, Victoire slipped on a *wòbakò* and crept into the kitchen. Around five, Maby and Délia, still fuddled with sleep, joined her and began filtering the coffee. Maby had replaced Flaminia, whom Boniface had finally sent back to Marie-Galante. Victoire insisted on preparing herself the *didiko* that Boniface took to his store on the quai Lardenoy for his ten o'clock break. It was her way of continuing to communicate with him. She knew he was fond of *blan manjé koko* and filled his meal tin with it. She then crossed the yard that was still in the shadows to the washroom reserved for the domestics.

The house on the rue de Nassau was one of the first to have running water, although other facilities were lacking for a long time to come. The WC, for example. Until 1920 the servants still decanted the contents of the *tomas* into the sanitary tubs during the predawn hours.

Victoire had always loved water. In La Pointe she took delight in discovering the rain. Not the quick shower immediately dried by the sun in Marie-Galante. But the never-ending rain that empties the streets; hammers on the zinc roofs; lashes against the persiennes, the verandas, the wrought iron of the balconies; refreshes the houses; and sprouts dreams in damp beds.

Naked, she would crouch against the rough wall of the stone basin above which dripped a tap. She would wash her long, straight hair that during the day she rolled into buns bristling with pins under her headtie. She would rub her body with a bunch of leaves, lingering over her private parts, surprised at the pleasure she felt. Already sovereign, the sun was climbing into the sky. She went back up to the room where Boniface, wide awake, still lazed in bed, and dressed for mass.

She then joined Anne-Marie at the foot of the stairs. The day they were to take communion they didn't have breakfast. Other times they drank coffee.

Outside, the sun was shining with its artful eye. The day was just beginning.

SEVEN

January 15, 1891, was a date to remember.

First of all, Boniface Walberg Jr., born nine months after Jeanne, was christened in the cathedral of Saint-Pierre and Saint-Paul in front of an assembly of white Creoles. Boniface Jr., who had inherited his mother's beauty, was nevertheless conceived under an unlucky star. His life went up in smoke like cigarette paper. Later in life, he married a white Creole from Dominica who died giving birth to their first child. Two years later he married a young girl who also died, from complications of an extrauterine pregnancy. After that he grew old on his own, sleeping with his maids.

Although I cannot prove it, I suspect he was strongly attracted to my mother, who returned the compliment without ever admitting it. He would have been only too keen to continue the tradition initiated by his father of sleeping with the Quidal women, but she refused. When she married my father, Boniface wrote to her as a frustrated lover accusing her of selling herself out to respectability. There was no doubt she didn't love the man she took for a husband. I don't know whether my mother ever answered his letter.

Second, on the occasion of this christening, Victoire's talent as a cook was revealed to one and all.

Why then?

Probably because Anne-Marie had had enough of the hostility that surrounded her only friend yet spared *her*. She wanted to thumb her nose at the narrow-mindedness and arrogance of polite society.

"I'll make them drool," she was heard to say.

Among the papers my mother kept was issue 51 of *L'Écho pointois*, where right in the middle of a laudatory article appears the menu for this christening banquet, lyrically composed like a poem and probably sent to the newspaper by Anne-Marie:

"The occasion was held at the Walbergs, a Roman feast, the work of a genuine Amphitryon. Judge for yourselves:

Black pudding stuffed with crayfish
Whelks on a bed of wild spinach and dasheen leaves
Lobster with green mangoes
Pork caramelized with aged rum and ginger
Rabbit fricassee with Bourbon oranges
Chayote gratin
Golden apple gratin
Green banana gratin
Purslane salad
Three sorbets: coconut, passion fruit, and lime
Creole gateau fouetté

What bold imagination, what creativity presided over the elaboration of these delights! Dear reader, isn't your mouth already watering?"

IN THOSE DAYS servants were passed around and exchanged like coins. They were borrowed and returned and never asked for their opinion or paid the slightest wage. From that day on Anne-Marie was bombarded with requests on visiting cards from the most eminent families. Could she loan Victoire for a christening, a birthday, or a wedding? Each time she had great pleasure replying in the negative. Since it is a well-known fact that desire is aroused if it is not reciprocated, Victoire's reputation increased with every refusal. Those who had disparaged her the most, in a total about-face, coveted her and dreamed of appropriating her for themselves.

Victoire did not appreciate the fuss made of her person. She reluctantly confided in Anne-Marie the secret of her culinary compositions so that the latter could name them and have them printed. As with a writer whose editor decides the title, cover, and illustrations of her book, it was partly like being dispossessed of her creation. She would have preferred to keep it secret. For her, cooking in no way implied wreaking vengeance on a society that had never made room for her. More than music, where she never excelled at playing the guitar or the flute, it was her way of expressing herself, which was constantly repressed, prisoner of her illiteracy, her illegitimacy, her gender, and her station as a servant. When she invented seasonings or blended flavors, her personality was set free and blossomed. Cooking was her Père Labat rum, her ganja, her crack, her ecstasy. She dominated the world. For a time she became God. Once again, like a writer.

We can of course imagine Anne-Marie and Victoire in collusion, sharing everything between them, where Anne-Marie would be called to the rescue to add the finishing touches to Victoire's culinary creation. But I refuse to believe anything of the sort. The creator is too jealous of her work to tolerate sharing. Victoire obeyed Anne-Marie grudgingly. Any information had to be dragged out of her.

Believing she was doing the right thing, Anne-Marie hired Francia, whose mission consisted of carrying out the unrewarding jobs that guarantee the perfection of a dish. But, as we said, Victoire did not tolerate any intruder in the temple where she officiated, and Francia didn't last long.

Every Friday evening the double doors of the grand living room were opened wide and the guests would surge in. A string quartet would get them dancing the *haute-taille* and the *réjane* until suppertime. But all that interested them was eating. Once dinner was served they did their best not to make a dash for the table. I have also found issue 55 of *L'Écho pointois*, where the menu of one of these dinners is published:

Shredded saltfish, smoked herring, and fresh tomatoes
Crayfish calalu
Whole sea bream marinated in limes
Turtle fricassee from Les Saintes
Indian rice
Cush-cush yam gratin
Heart of cabbage tree salad
Chodo custard
Gateau fouetté

To TELL THE truth, these weekly receptions, which were a pretext to show off gold chokers and the latest fashion from Paris, were an ordeal for Anne-Marie as well. The only avenging pleasure she felt was when the guests clapped their hands in frenzy, calling for Victoire. She would appear, swallowed up in a beige apron embroidered with a grill, an allusion to Saint Lawrence, patron saint of cooks, her cheeks flushed from the attention, then dart back into her refuge.

All this was also displeasing to Boniface, the least sociable of men, whose only subject of conversation was the price of a barrel of saltfish. Furthermore, we can assume that he was unhappy seeing his Victoire exhibited like a fairground attraction, gifted though she was. Consequently, he took his courage in both hands and informed Anne-Marie that it was causing too much expense. Just the drinks were exorbitant! He backed up his grievances by listing the cost of the brandy, aged rum, anisette from Bordeaux, and gin she gave to her guests. Cursing his miserliness, Anne-Marie, whose dowry, lest we forget, brought neither a bank account, property, nor country estate, had to accept.

The receptions came to an end. The operation, whose point was to crown Victoire with prestige, had failed. The recently created association of cooks did in fact offer her the honorary presidency. But she declined the offer, which was felt as an insult.

Pursuing my comparison, like many writers and artists, Victoire cared little for recognition by the Other. On the contrary, her shyness made her cherish her anonymity. Cooking was her way of satisfying an inner need.

IN THE MEANTIME, Jeanne was growing up.

She spoke Creole only with her mother, since Anne-Marie forbade speaking this jargon under her roof, even with the servants. They should be addressed in French. They would jabber as best they could in reply.

Ever since Jeanne was seven or eight, her skin had darkened to a deep brown, which was surprising if you think of Victoire's color. Likewise, her hair, first curly then curled tight like an Arab shepherd's, turned frizzy and kinky while remaining thick and long. In this color-obsessed society, did she suffer from being so different from her mother, from having come out the "wrong" color? I haven't a clue. Throughout her life she made a point of despising the light-skinned *peaux-chappées*, rewriting in her manner the Song of Songs:

> I am black and I am beautiful, O daughters of Jerusalem,
> Black as the tents of Kedar
> As the curtains of Solomon.

Everyone concurred that she was cold, aloof, and not at all agreeable. She talked very little and smiled even less. Always impassive, she tolerated without blinking the strangest situations. At mealtimes, she would take her place at the oval table in the dining room that was covered in crystal, porcelain, and silverware. Meanwhile, her mother would be busy serving the meal before eating with her hands out of a calabash on her lap in the yard. Jeanne would wash in the children's bathroom using perfumed soap, talcum powder, and lotion, whereas her mother rubbed her own body down with a clump of straw in the servants' washhouse. Thanks to Anne-Marie, who once a quarter drew up a list of items to be ordered from the department stores in Paris, Jeanne wore dresses, shoes, and hats in the latest fashion, whereas her mother in headtie went barefoot or wore slippers and shapeless *golle* dresses. Since Anne-Marie disliked the promiscuity of school, although it was reserved for white children, the destitute widow of a former plantation owner, Mme. de Saunier du Val, came to teach Jeanne as well as Boniface Jr. the rudiments of reading and writing. What never ceases to surprise me is that mother and daughter didn't make use of the occasion to share the same alphabet primer, Jeanne teaching Victoire the alphabet, both of them making mistakes, reciting and deciphering the letters together, and that Victoire remained illiterate as before. Was she ashamed of putting herself on the same level as her daughter? Was she afraid of Mme. Saunier du Val, hardly affable, like all those who have suffered a reversal of fortune? Whatever the case, she missed an opportunity to remedy a flaw that afflicted her throughout her life.

La bayè ba, sé là bèf ka janbé. There where the fence is down, the bull jumps through. Creole proverb.

The servants who feared and were jealous of Victoire did not dare take it out on her. Instead, they took their revenge on her little girl. Flaminia burnt her on the shoulder with an iron. She bore this mark all her life. Her relations with the rest of the household were not simple. With Boniface Jr. especially, they were always ambiguous. Sometimes capricious and cantankerous, he took the side of the servants, calling her an intruder and a bastard. Other times, he defended her against their sarcasm and stifled her with kisses and caresses. I don't know how far they went. But I believe she was always wary of him as if he stood for danger. Since she did not have an ear for music, Anne-Marie chose to ignore her. Her own mother apparently had no time for her, too busy praying to God, listening to music, or cooking. The only person left who constantly showed her any affection was *Bèf pòtoriko*, although she never called him by any name other than Monsieur Walberg.

How I would like to include here a case of pedophilia! The white Creole swine abusing the little Negro girl, his servant's daughter. Alas! Boniface Walberg was a modest man of integrity. He would enter Jeanne's bedroom simply to read her a bedtime story and then make the sign of the cross on her forehead. He would spoil her as if she were his own daughter, returning home from the quai Lardenoy with his pockets filled with *siwo* candy, *grabyo koko*, and sweet corn *kilibibi*. At carnival time he would take her onto the Place de la Victoire to admire the masqueraders wearing toques. For her fifth birthday he gave her a marionette, a *bwa bwa*, dressed in a striped suit, wearing a crown, whose arms and legs moved when you pulled the strings. She began to hate him at the age of eleven because she discovered the nature of his relations with her mother. One stormy night, streaked with lightning and booming with the stentorian voice of thunder, she took refuge in the Regency room and found him asleep in Victoire's arms with the sheet thrown back, exhibiting his monstrous private parts.

Soon everything changed. The ambient hypocrisy, harassment, and indifference no longer had any importance. Jeanne discovered what was going to matter in her life: her studies. Mme. de Saunier du Val, who had served her time, was replaced by M. Roumegoux, who came every morning to give private lessons. This illegitimate son of a white Creole and an Indian mother, a former seminarian, who had been terrified by the vows of chastity, had been hired by Anne-Marie on the basis of an advertisement in *L'Écho pointois*: "Young man who has studied at Pau, of illegitimate birth but belonging to a well-established and reputable family, seeks position in a family who would appreciate his extensive knowledge. Likes

Mozart, Johann Sebastian Bach, and Offenbach. Untalented player of the violin, recorder, and lute."

Since the nursery was no longer big enough, she fitted out a room with somewhat disparate furniture: a large writing desk with three drawers, a Directoire bookcase, and four or five chairs in the Louis XVI style. M. Roumegoux sat his bony buttocks in an armchair of the same style and the lesson began:

"The world is comprised of five continents: Africa, Asia, Oceania, the Americas, and Europe.

"Africa doesn't count. Over there is a bunch of savages and cannibals who eat one another in a cooking pot. Asia and Oceania are not much better. The armies of Alexander the Great, who was the first to enter India, brought back stories of people who instead of burying their dead devoured them alive. There was a time when the Americas were mistaken for an earthly paradise, the Garden of Eden. Amerigo Vespucci writes in a famous letter dated 1500 to Lorenzo di Pierfrancesco de Medici: 'It is true that if there is an earthly paradise somewhere in this world, I believe it cannot be far from these lands.'

"In the end they discovered that here too was nothing but a place of barbarity. All that is left is Europe. Situated at the center of the world, Europe is the heir and apex of classical civilization. Ever since the fifteenth century, since the Renaissance, it has constantly generated a torrent of fertilizing ideas. We have witnessed a genuine passion for knowledge and the greatest expansion of the arts ever seen. In the eyes of its philosophers, there is nothing more admirable than Man."

Jeanne swallowed all that hook, line, and sinker, and M. Roumegoux marveled at her intelligence.

"You could go far. Pity you're so black!" he sighed, caressing what Boniface Jr. in one of his bad days had christened with the name of a cactus commonly found on La Désirade and known for its spines: "Englishman's head."

On May 12, 1898, a daughter by the name of Valérie-Anne was

born at the home of the Walbergs. I have no idea how Boniface strayed into the bed of Anne-Marie, since the only words that passed between them were on the subject of the household accounts. Was he drunk that night, because sometimes he did drink to excess the aged Martinican rum Crassoul de Médoul, and went in the wrong door? We shall never know. Anne-Marie's unwanted pregnancy was terrible. She lay bedridden from beginning to end. Vertigo. Nausea. Vomiting. Both legs swollen like tree trunks. What's more, the infant had the misfortune of inheriting the freckles and red hair of an Irish ancestor.

"Good Lord, she's so ugly!" exclaimed her mother, pushing her away when the midwife tried to lay her on her breast. "Nine months of torture to give birth to that!"

We are told that a newborn hears these words, and all through her life never forgets them as well as the person who pronounced them.

In order to hide her red hair, they called upon the services of a dressmaker, who fashioned lawn and linen bonnets resembling the headdress of the women in Saint-Barth. Henceforth, there was someone more mocked and forlorn than Jeanne, who now had somebody to console. For a time Valérie-Anne snuggled up under her wing. Then she snuggled under Victoire's when the latter, finding herself removed from her daughter, felt as forsaken as Valérie-Anne.

Sometimes the ill-treated take their revenge. Still a teenager, Valérie-Anne married the son of a rich banana planter from the region of Saint-Claude who was rolling in money. At the end of her life it was rumored that her jewel box weighed forty pounds. She bore five sons, one of whom became a monk.

As an adult, she would never go near my mother. Both of them hated each other.

EIGHT

O ne evening in April, shortly after sunset, the sky was ablaze
with a glow through the persiennes.

"Yet another fire," said Boniface, coming out onto the balcony in
his pajamas without bothering to slip on his dressing gown. "Fortunately we have nothing to fear, since the wind isn't blowing in our
direction."

He calmly went back to bed, where Victoire, rolled up in a ball,
was waiting for him. They made love two or three times as they usually did each night.

The next morning La Pointe awoke amid the sound and the fury.
Surging in from the outlying districts, the *maléré* had invaded the
center of town. Groups of ragged individuals were gathering at the
crossroads and filling the sidewalks, sobbing and moaning noisily.

The event was major.

At the age of thirty-eight Dernier Argilius had just perished in
the fire that had broken out the night before at the offices of the
newspaper *Le Peuple*. Apart from the rue Henri IV, the rue Barbès, the rue Sadi-Carnot, and a good part of the rue Schoelcher had
been destroyed. If Jean-Hégésippe Légitimus had not been at the
National Assembly in Paris, where he was a representative, they

would have been mourning the assassination of two leaders, since the people's anger had been aroused by the fact that this fire had been set on purpose by the white Creole factory owners. Under the pretext of political instability, their objective was to call the United States of America to the rescue and turn Guadeloupe into another Cuba or Puerto Rico. For the *maléré*, oblivious of the vicissitudes of sugar, enemy number one was M. Ernest Souques, owner of the Darboussier and Bellevue factories, and shareholder in the companies at Port-Louis and Sainte-Anne. In fact, it wouldn't have taken much for them to accuse him of striking the match himself.

Victoire heard the news from the milk seller who came by every day at six thirty on the dot, balancing her tray of bottles on her head. As usual, she did not show any emotion and took in the news without blinking. Then, untying her apron, she went upstairs to dress. In the bedroom she held her head between both hands: when she was sixteen this man who had just perished had initiated her into sex. He had been neither tender nor affectionate. He would possess her brutally without a word, withdraw as soon as it was over, light a horrible Brazilian cigar, and, completely naked, bury himself in the newspaper. Sometimes, he would write an article. His Sergent-Major pen, dipped in mauve ink, scratched over the paper. He would look up only when the door creaked and she left to go.

"See you tomorrow!" he growled roughly.

It was an order, an assessment of his power.

"*Silplètadyé!* God willing!" she murmured.

Nevertheless, she had taken pleasure in his arms and conceived. For the first and last time. As a sign of mourning she chose a black *golle* dress with white polka dots and a mauve headtie.

Passing the bedroom door of Anne-Marie, who was writing to Rochelle or Etienne, Victoire was tempted to inform her of Dernier's death. But she guessed the caustic remarks she would make:

"One bastard less! The world will be better off without him. For goodness' sake, you're not going to shed tears over *him*!"

So she merely murmured through the wooden door:

"*Mwen kale*. I'm off."

It's always a surprise that the weather is beautiful when the heart is hurting or in distress. Outside, the sun was shining yellow in a blue sky washed of clouds. Gathering pollen from roses in the gardens and hibiscus in the hedgerows, the hummingbirds outdid one another with their trills. The western neighborhood of the town was a heap of smoldering, charred planks and corrugated iron. Since the rue Henri IV was nothing more than ashes and rubble, Dernier's remains had been carried to one of his aunts, on the rue des Abymes. A sizable crowd was cluttering up the sidewalk, since he had been the darling of those who distrusted Légitimus. Wasn't the latter colluding with the enemy, the white Creole factory owners? In actual fact, their fears were not unfounded. A few years later, Légitimus was to sit down at the same table as Ernest Souques to sign the Capital-Work agreement, considered by historians, except for Jean-Pierre Sainton, as treason.

People looked Victoire up and down. Where did this mulatto woman spring from? Who was she wearing mourning for? What was she after? A whiplash from a *zambo*? There were quite a few among the mourners. But given her determined look, they drew back and let her in.

Dernier had been so disfigured by his burns that out of respect for the family he had immediately been placed in a coffin away from the public gaze. In the only bedroom it was quite a crush. His family, a genuine tribe of picky head country bumpkins from Marie-Galante, was in tears. An aunt firmly held a bottle of volatile alcali under the nose of Dernier's mother, who was on the verge of fainting. Since he had been a Freemason, members of the Egalitarians' Masonic Lodge of Freethinkers complete with hats and black suits were swaggering next to the more slovenly looking representatives of the Republican Youth Committee and the Social Studies Club. There were a great many women. Uniformly dressed in garnet-colored dresses with leg-of-mutton sleeves, they belonged to the association of the True Daughters of Schoelcher. Numerous kids too, claiming to represent the association the Children of Marianne. Except for the latter, everyone was drinking heavily and the level of rum in the demijohns was getting dangerously low. Those who had had the most to drink were sobbing shamelessly.

At 2 p.m. the din of conch horns could be heard, belonging to the strapping Negroes over six feet tall from the Socialist Federation of the Grands-Fonds, whom everyone feared. They took charge of the coffin, shifting it from one shoulder to the other, then set off for the cemetery, for Dernier had never had time for the church's holy sacraments. Like all the socialists at that time, he was violently anti-clerical and wrote in *Le Peuple* that religion was man's stupidity.

The funeral cortege was unending. The Workers' Chorale, who opened the procession chanting socialist hymns, was threading its way between the graves, dug at ground level and marked out by the white rocks of the Bergevin graveyard, while the tail end of the cortege was still trailing along the rue des Abymes. Almost right up until evening, in front of the open grave, following the hymns, came a series of speeches that all expressed the same despair. Ah, the mold was broken. There wouldn't be men of that caliber anymore.

Victoire listened. She wondered what her life would have been like if Dernier's passion for the disinherited had materialized into an interest for her own destitution. If this *vayan nèg*, this valiant Negro, who had advocated free schooling for all, had taken her hand to decipher the letters of the alphabet. Does caring for the forest prevent you from looking after each and every one of its trees? What else does love for humanity signify if not love and respect for every human being? That is why deep down in her heart when she thought of Dernier she felt an immense bitterness. She couldn't help thinking that it was the hand of justice that had lit the fire.

Night had fallen when she arrived back at the rue de Nassau.

It was an evening of *entente cordiale*. Boniface Jr. had joined in Jeanne and Valérie-Anne's games. The three children were running after one another in the back garden, uttering Siouxlike shouts. Victoire drew her daughter against her and to Jeanne's great surprise kissed her. Such a show of affection was rare. She was tempted to tell her:

"Papa w sòti mò."

But had her father in fact just died? For her, hadn't he died before she was born, nine years earlier, when, without bothering to tell a soul, he had boarded the steamship and put an ocean between himself and two women with whom he had gone through the gestures of lovemaking?

She kept silent. But from that moment on she took Jeanne to the cemetery at Bergevin every All Saints' Day. The socialists had clubbed together to give Dernier the tomb he deserved: a ponderous monument of cement and freestone. There was always a crowd around it, praying, lighting candles, changing the water in the vases, and replacing the wilted wreaths and bouquets with fresh flowers; a crowd of inconsolable individuals uttering heartrending cries. Jeanne had no idea why she was there. While her mother knelt down on the cold stone and lost herself in prayer (what was she asking God for?), Jeanne told herself stories to kill time. All she had to do was look around her. Trees everywhere. Flamboyants of an indecent red. Casuarinas. Mango trees loaded with fruit that nobody dared fight over with the dead. The number of funeral processions entering the gates impressed her. It was as if the inhabitants of La Pointe were dying like flies. Here a well-dressed, even opulent-looking, light-skinned family was following a small white coffin. A child. Their child? A daughter? A son? Born into happiness and great expectations. A christening awash with *chodo* custard and *gateau fouetté*. Death does not spare the affluent.

A few alleys over, next to a grove of mango trees, a black family in tears was burying Linda, the apple of their eye: 1880–1899. Committed suicide out of love. The man she worshipped had abandoned her. So she gulped down a massive dose of tincture of laudanum. Commit suicide for a man? What stupidity! As for Death, she didn't need much persuading; she'll make do with any prey.

When the chicken hawks began to spread their wings in the night air, the tombs would be glowing from the candles lit by an infinity of devoted hands. Her mother stood up, dusted off her knees, and led her by the hand back to the rue de Nassau. This protective gesture no longer made much sense. The daughter had recently grown taller and bigger than her mother.

Jeanne ended up guessing why year after year Victoire took her to this grave, and she understood that Dernier Argilius must be her father. She took no pride in the fact. There is no reason why she should have. She mentioned it to nobody and never sought to make herself known to his family. The fact that he abandoned her mother, that he never for one moment bothered about the fruit of her womb, and let her, Jeanne, grow up in the charitable care of a family of white Creoles seemed to her the perfect illustration of this male tendency to maintain a heroic posture without assuming the real human duties that are often obscure and insignificant.

Dernier Argilius was nothing but a whited sepulcher.

Without seeking to excuse him, one question remains, however: Did he know about his daughter? Did Victoire have the courage to confess to him her condition? This presupposes an intimacy that perhaps never existed between them. He took her, withdrew, and went his way. He never asked questions, and not being very talkative, she never confided in him. However, even if he had been aware of her pregnancy, it is unlikely that Jeanne's destiny would have changed. Up till very recently our men were like sowers, carelessly sowing the first field they came across. Sociology and literature are full of stories illustrating this machismo. "The condition of the Antillean woman" has become an indispensable topic of interviews, dissertations, and theses.

All that is in the process of changing, like Antillean society itself. What will our American students have to write about in the coming years?

NINE

I have described in *Tales from the Heart: True Stories from my Childhood* how nobody in my family told me anything about slavery or the slave trade, those initiatory voyages that founded our Caribbean destiny. I had to negotiate on my own the weight of this terrible past. On the other hand, since individual stories have replaced our collective history, my mother on several occasions alluded to a journey my grandmother (whom she seldom mentioned except for a few clichés) made to Martinique in the year 1901. I keep asking myself why she insisted. What did she want to tell me? Her watered-down version of this modest odyssey took up the home-sweet-home theme, so beloved of the English, illustrating the risks an honest woman ran by leaving the security of her own home; by having adventures with men who respect nothing and nobody; by undergoing physical ordeals and leaving herself vulnerable to suffering, degeneration, and death. When I think about it, I believe it was her way of exorcising a memory whose pain never subsided. In actual fact, as a result of this journey, her mother met a stranger and abandoned Guadeloupe and her daughter for him. It didn't matter that she recovered her wits and returned home, the intention was there. It was proof that her daughter did not mean everything to her.

The facts I managed to gather corroborate my mother's fears. This journey and the distress it caused can be considered incendiary and excusable, when all is said and done, in a life that was routine to say the least. Victoire, who at the time was only twenty-eight, that age when body and heart are raging with desire, was tempted to rearrange her lifeline. I can equate her flight with one of those types of marooning of which Victor Schoelcher speaks when the African, tired of the rigors of slavery, dreams of freedom but lacks the determination needed to realize his plans.

Here are the facts.

Those who are called local whites in Guadeloupe and *Békés* in Martinique amount to one and the same creature. Since the sixteenth century identical names can be found on either side of the Caribbean Sea. In 1684, Donatien Walberg, having sliced up a rival with a machete—they were both sharing the same bed of a free colored woman without knowing it—fled Guadeloupe in a fishing boat. Quite by chance, he sailed up a river and settled in Le Francois in the south of Martinique. There he founded a family. One of his descendants, Philimond, a merchant at Saint-Pierre, married Amélie Desgranges in February 1901. Philimond had spent many of his childhood vacations with the branch of his family in Marie-Galante and was especially fond of his cousin Boniface, who, like him, had succeeded in business. He therefore invited Boniface together with his wife to his wedding, specifying that they should bring with them their cook, whose reputation had reached far beyond the shores of the island.

Leaving the household in charge of the servants, Boniface and Anne-Marie, flanked by Victoire, succumbing under the weight of the wicker baskets that supplemented three large trunks, settled into the first-class section of the *Lusitania* for an eight-hour crossing. The steamer had barely left the quai Foulon when Anne-Marie began to feel sick. A little later she began to vomit noisily into brown paper bags. The sight of this woman bent in two, a greenish bile around her lips, was not very inviting, so Boniface went and stretched his legs on the promenade deck.

Ever since Victoire had left Marie-Galante some ten years earlier with her infant in her arms, she had never crossed the high seas. The immensity of the voyage they were about to undertake frightened her. At the slightest noise or rolling movement she imagined the *Lusitania* swallowed up by the waves. More harrowing than this physical fear, though, were the thoughts that the wind on the open sea fanned like glowing embers. Jeanne had just been admitted to the Sisters of Saint-Joseph-de-Cluny day school, which had opened its doors right behind the church. This solid edifice built of gray stone still exists. It was not one of those schools founded strictly for the education of white girls. They accepted colored girls as well, most of them mulattoes from well-to-do families. According to some indiscreet revelations, Jeanne apparently was the class punching bag. Using little imagination, the pupils nicknamed her Little Whitey. One of their favorite ways of greeting her every morning was to dance round her, singing a nursery rhyme:

> *A little Negress who was drinking some milk*
> *Said to herself, oh if only I could dip my head in a bowl*
>   *of milk*
> *I'd become whiter*
> *Than all the French, my, my, my.*

She herself never complained. She merely became increasingly remote, increasingly silent, a foreigner to all those around her. As if she came from elsewhere, as if she possessed her own untranslatable idiom and her own incommunicable ways. Anne-Marie shrugged her shoulders:

"Pooh! It will forge her character. Whoever we are, we all have to get over our childhood."

Victoire did not contradict her. Yet *a pa vré sa* (that's not true), she thought, head lowered over her tomato coulis. Her childhood had been her only moment of happiness. She felt terrible for Jeanne and tortured herself, realizing that perhaps she had made a huge mistake believing she had acted for her daughter's good. Daughter of a servant to a white Creole family, wasn't that a scar that would remain with her all life long? She wondered how else she could ensure her education and contribute to the blossoming of her intellectual gifts.

Around eleven, since Anne-Marie's vomiting had subsided, she went and joined Boniface, who was calmly leaning against the ship's rail, scanning the immense horizon. His serenity had a calming effect on her. Her fears appeared laughable to him. She convinced herself he was right. As long as he was alive, she possessed the security that Jeanne needed. Security, that's the main thing.

At times, schools of flying fish sheathed in silver like shining commas leapt out of the water. At a respectful distance a procession of porpoises accompanied them. Apart from that, blue waves rippled as far as the eye could see. Apart from that, there was nothing else. Nothing.

Although they had left at dawn, when they arrived at Fort-de-France, night had fallen. They could not make out much of the bay, one of the most beautiful in the world, whatever Césaire might think. The town, which like La Pointe was a constant victim of conflagrations, hurricanes, and earthquakes, appeared sad and haggard. The unfortunate coaling girls, described with a dubious lyricism by Lafcadio Hearn, were bent double under their loads as they filed up the gangways of a steamer belonging to the Compagnie Générale Transatlantique bound for Bordeaux. Women carrying water jars waddled along one behind another. Boniface, Anne-Marie, and Victoire ignored the line of carriages for hire and walked. Unlike La Pointe, where walking was a perilous exercise because of the pickpockets, beggars, piles of garbage, and all sorts of clutter, the streets of Fort-de-France were practically deserted. The municipality had just renamed them and they bore the names of contemporary writers: Victor Hugo, Schoelcher, Isambert, and Perrinon. To save money, Boniface took a room for three in the Hotel du Prince Alfred. The window opened onto the oasis of tamarind and mango trees on the Savane. According to a tradition recently revived, the oompah-oompah of a band could be heard. They were playing *La Belle Hélène* by Offenbach. For one moment Anne-Marie was tempted to look for a bench, sit down, and listen. But she was utterly worn-out, like Boniface and Victoire. The trio did not even have the strength to go and admire the statue of the Empress Joséphine de Beauharnais, which had just been erected and nobody had yet thought of slashing her neck. Cutthroat statue. They retired for the night.

In what manner of fashion?

The moon in her curiosity peeked through the persiennes, but there was nothing ambiguous to see, if only to reveal the social hierarchy of the time.

Out of respect for the two women, Boniface removed only his patent leather shoes and jacket. He lay down practically fully dressed on the bench, set beside the bow-fronted armoire, and immediately filled the room with his snores. Anne-Marie slipped on her batiste nightdress. Propped up against her pillows, she began to read *L'Imitation de Notre Seigneur Jésus-Christ*. She had put on quite a bit of weight, a genuine Rubens, blonde and pink. She blamed her portliness on Victoire's sumptuous cooking and her irrepressible sweet tooth, especially for the *rahat-loukoum* they sold at the patisserie Trébert. Victoire, sitting at the very edge of the bed, undid her headtie and removed one by one the pins that held her buns, releasing her long black hair. Then, in her burlap nightdress as rough as a flour sack from France, she flopped down onto the patch of carat palm mat between the bed and the bench. Around midnight Anne-Marie woke her for a body friction with camphorated alcohol. She wasn't feeling too well.

The wedding took place at Le François on the family estate. They traveled in a hired "family-size" carriage. Today the Walberg sugar plantation is a famous landmark. It has been transformed by an enterprising heir into a five-star hotel. Tourists book certain rooms months in advance, insisting they sleep in the former slave shacks. Although these have been updated, they are a reminder of a past age.

At that time the plantation produced its bushels of sugar year in, year out. The wedding of Philimond and Amélie, which it was hosting, was what is commonly called a beautiful wedding. For the marriage ceremony, three hundred and fifty guests, most of them from Saint-Pierre, crowded into the church, destroyed in 1891 by a hurricane that had killed sixty people, and rebuilt on the spot miraculously designated in a vision by one of the nuns of a neighboring convent. The wedding banquet was served on tables laid out in the plantation yard illuminated *a giorno* by torchères. Two orchestras that were a hit in the cabarets of Saint-Pierre, commonly cited as the uncontested capital of good taste, continued playing fashionable melodies one after another while waiting for the ball to open in the former boiling house. They would dance the cotillion and the cake walk imported from America until dawn. They would also sashay to the sounds of the beguine that was all the rage from one end of the island to the other:

Manman, mwen desann Sèn Pyè

In order to satisfy the desires of all these guests who were living their final days without knowing it, about twenty domestics had been laboring since dawn in the disused mill, transformed into a kitchen. Victoire was not afraid of the competition by the caterers, who'd also come from Saint-Pierre, with their guinea fowl stew. She was preparing one of her culinary triumphs, duck cooked in cassava and lemongrass—which I came across quite by chance years later in Belem—when a handsome Negro, somewhat of a dandy in his tight-fitting dark jacket, approached Victoire. She had met his insistent eyes with a beating heart several times. Once, he had even purposely brushed up against her. His name was Alexandre Arconte and he was the wine waiter, or in other words the employee in charge of drinks lent by O'Lanyer and Sons from Saint-Pierre and supervising a host of waiters skilled at pouring aperitifs, white wine, red wine, champagne, and liqueurs stored in the vinegar cellar. Victoire was red and sweating from the heat of the bagasse and kindling, which for economy's sake had replaced the charcoal. Consequently, he placed a glass of orange wine between her hands, which she gratefully accepted.

"Just look at them!" he murmured, not budging. "Has anything changed since the days of slavery? They're having the time of their lives, whereas we are working ourselves to death."

She vaguely sensed the truth in his words. For Victoire, who had always worked without ever possessing anything, without ever receiving anything in return, who could neither read nor write, who lived off the goodwill of a white family, the abolition of slavery had changed absolutely nothing.

What would happen if she quit her collar, she asked herself once again? She could become a street seller and sell popular dishes such as rice and beans, fried fish and court bouillon. Or else become a hawker, toting merchandise from village to village, far from the main marketplaces. Difficult and exhausting work that frightened her. Was she lacking in courage?

She did not know what to say. Apparently Alexandre was not offended by her silence, since he invited her to sip a glass of Dutch anisette with him. A few hours later, when couples slipped their arms around each other's waist and with wings on their heels flew to the ballroom, inquisitive eyes followed them as they delved into the park's thick vegetation. I imagine it was something like the beginning of the world: acres of woodland lush with casuarinas, trumpet bushes, cigar-box cedars, palms and silk cotton trees, crisscrossed by forest paths and tracks running in every direction. If you followed those to the south, you came to the sea and a gentle beach strewn with shells and seaweed.

Anne-Marie was the first to sound the alarm when the morning after the wedding her faithful Victoire did not tap on her door. She had to wash her hair herself. As for the caterers, waiters, and employees of O'Lanyer and Sons who embarked on the *Topaze* for Saint-Pierre at the end of the afternoon, they noticed that Alexandre was missing and had to set sail without him.

On the evening of the fourth day, those who remained in the vicinity of Le François organized a search party for the missing couple. In vain. Boniface looked a sorry sight. His grief even softened the heart of Anne-Marie, who dabbed his tears like a maman.

"*Bon dyé!*" he gasped. "O Lord, if she dies, I die too."

"Who's talking about dying?" she berated him.

Anne-Marie decided not to leave, which put her hosts in a predicament, since they were anxious to get back to Saint-Pierre. She did not know how she would explain Victoire's absence on her return to La Pointe and imagined all sorts of lies in her head: Victoire had wandered off into the woods and been bitten by a poisonous trigonocephale snake. The thick groves around the Walberg plantation were swarming with them. Most unlikely. Let's try something else: Victoire had been tempted by the offer of a restaurant owner who had proposed a small fortune for her to work in the kitchen. Quite implausible too. So what could she invent?

After almost two weeks, her hosts were at the end of their tether and she had to resign herself to set off back home again with Boniface.

Back on the rue de Nassau, she briefly explained to Jeanne in disbelief that her mother was staying in Martinique for a time. Then, clutching her to her heart, she burst into tears, which had the effect of terrifying the child. What was her mother doing in Martinique? She must be dead and they were afraid to tell her. Jeanne began imagining Victoire carried away by a huge wave or struck by lightning or crushed by a tree.

Life resumed its usual routine.

Or almost.

By way of letters from friends and relatives in Martinique, the affair soon reached the ears of the bourgeois circle of harpies in La Pointe, who gleefully badmouthed Victoire. They let fly at her, calling her *bòbò*, slut, a debauched individual, and a heartless mother who disrespected respectable households at the most sacred of times. At the sisters' day school, Jeanne heard snatches of these stories, each more revolting than the last. The nuns pretended to take pity on her and were lavish with their consolation. Their compassion, however, was worse than their contempt.

Fortunately, back home, it was another story.

Here again I have nothing juicy to offer. Under the white skins of Anne-Marie and Boniface, deep down beat the heart of a normal man and woman. Both fretted about the poor abandoned child.

"We shall have to tell her the truth in the end," sighed Anne-Marie.

"Wait a bit! She'll come back!" maintained Boniface, who wanted to keep hope alive. Despite the odds. Despite the silence and the passing months.

They did not think for one moment of abusing or abandoning her. On the contrary! They were more considerate toward her than ever, especially Anne-Marie. At Christmas they gave her a gold bangle, her first jewel.

Polite society had begun to forget about Victoire, who had disappeared for over a year, when one fine morning with a wicker basket on her head she pushed open the door to the house on the rue de Nassau and quite simply cried out "I'm back" to the stunned servants:

"Mi mwen."

She went up to the Regency room to unpack her things without bothering to answer Anne-Marie, who was bombarding her with questions. At noon, contrary to habit, she went to fetch her child from school. Jeanne, who had recently dreamed of her mother turning purple from being suffocated by a boa constrictor around her neck, saw her suddenly turn up at the gate, surprisingly spruce, the mask of a young girl tacked onto her face. She almost ran to embrace her but, taking control of herself, merely asked how she was:

"Ou bien mèsi?"

As a result, tongues started wagging again. Some vital information was passed on. It was rumored that Alexandre Arconte was not what he made himself out to be. Instead of an upstairs-downstairs house, he possessed merely a modest two-room shack. Instead of a tidy sum in the bank, he hadn't a penny to his name. Venal Victoire had real-ized her mistake. Beauty does not put food on the table. Leave Boni-face for this fly-by-night? Reason had taken the upper hand.

These events had a tragic epilogue.

Less than two weeks after Victoire returned home, on May 8, 1902, Mount Pelée started belching fire. With a wave of her magic wand, the wicked fairy turned the pearl of the Antilles into the ghost town visited today by tourists and souvenir hunters. Not one survivor, except for Cyparis, saved by his solitary confinement. Among the thirty thousand victims of the catastrophe there were Philimond and his young bride, most of the wedding guests, the musicians, the caterers, the domestics, and Alexandre. If she had stayed with him in Martinique, Victoire would have suffered the same fate.

Boniface and Anne-Marie had trouble getting over the fact that a year earlier they had danced with a group of *morituri,* whereas Victoire got the impression of having escaped the arms of a cadaver. She never forgave herself for having left Alexandre when the most terrible danger was looming behind him. Night after night she saw herself making love to a mummy who unwound his bandages one by one, revealing a putrescent flesh. She believed too that she had been punished for having abandoned her daughter for so long. In short, she was in agony. On May 20, 1902, Anne-Marie sent Etienne a letter containing this terse sentence: "Only her faith in God is keeping our faithful Victoire alive."

I hardly need say that this little-known, badly elucidated incident aroused my curiosity to the fullest. Although we know for sure that Philimond Walberg and his wife perished together with the aris-tocracy of Saint-Pierre, that the offices of O'Lanyer and Sons, rue Victor Hugo, were destroyed from top to bottom, there is nothing to prove that Alexander was in town on that day. Perhaps by chance, with the help of good luck, he had traveled to Fort-de-France or Le François on business the day before or the day before that. My task proved to be arduous. All I could find in the newspapers of that time, archived in the Schoelcher Library in Fort-de-France, were advertisements for wines and liquors by O'Lanyer, father and son. No mention of Alexandre Arconte. I was about to give up my research when a student from Martinique working on one of my books sent me an e-mail. Her name: Denise Arconte.

Yes, Alexandre was the elder brother of her grandfather, who unfortunately perished in the catastrophe. She had no information of a possible liaison with a girl from Guadeloupe. She thought he was married to a certain Louise Girondin, who, together with their three children, had perished with him. At the most she knew he owned a restaurant in Saint-Pierre called Le Gargantua, something quite unusual for the time, when tourism was unheard of and people ate at home. My research turned up nothing on Le Gargantua.

All that we have left is our imagination.

One evening I pushed open the door to Le Gargantua. Modest. Not much room. Background music: Martinican beguines—"Bavaroise," "Marie-Clémence," "Agoulou." Five or six tables occupied by some sailors from Venezuela. Alexandre carries his virility proudly with prominent attributes. I look at the menu. Prix fixe. Fairly simple.

Cream of pumpkin soup with garlic and shrimps
Stuffed chayotes
Grilled sea bream on saffron rice
Salad of spinach shoots
Coconut sorbet

Without a smile and dressed in the Martinican mode, Victoire is assiduously serving the dishes from table to table and removing the plates. At times, she goes over to Alexandre and they talk in low murmurs. He whispers the orders to her as if they are a secret.

Afterward, amid the rumbling of the volcano, they frenziedly make love.

TEN

This long elopement had little effect on the relations between Victoire, Anne-Marie, and Boniface. Anne-Marie had an unending supply of romanticism that justified falling in love at first sight, something that she—alas!—had never done. She lived the passion through the intermediary of Victoire and reconstituted the affair in her imagination, since Victoire did not tell her very much.

After months of blinding love, the thought of her beloved Jeanne must have haunted Victoire. She ended up confessing to Alexandre, who went into a rage. How dare she keep secrets from him! Why should he look after this papaless child? It would be like eating someone's leftovers. She let the storm subside, then returned to the attack. He was inflexible. She ended up leaving.

On the ship back home, she almost threw herself into the sea a hundred times. When the shores of Guadeloupe came into view, she wanted to die. Suddenly her decision to return seemed absurd. She was sacrificing herself for a child who would soon have a life of her own, from which perhaps she would be ruthlessly excluded.

Boniface, who was only too happy to get back a body to which he was so attached, forgave everything. He never put the slightest blame on Victoire, content merely to ask her from time to time with a pathetic humility:

"Kon sa, ou té òbliyé mwen?" (You never thought of me once all that time?)

It was shortly afterward, however, that relations between Victoire and Jeanne started to deteriorate seriously. Okay, they had never been very demonstrative. Neither of them seemed apt at those out-pourings of tenderness that are natural between a mother and her only daughter. Yet a type of subterranean communication bound them one to the other like a secret passageway. From one day to the next all that ceased, replaced by a muted hostility, at least in Jeanne. It was expressed by mere nothings. Jeanne no longer allowed her mother to dress her and do her hair. She combed her hair as best she could with a mixture of water and castor oil and tied it in a bow on her neck. She picked out and slipped on her panties all by her-self. Worse still, she who previously had a healthy appetite began to eat like a sparrow. In a single month she consequently lost twenty pounds, signifying therefore that she wanted nothing to do with earthly nourishment, as a way of punishing her mother, who placed so much importance on it. In a manner of speaking she refused any type of dialogue with her. At the same time, she professed to loathe music, especially Bach, Vivaldi, and Italian operas; in short, all the favorites of Anne-Marie and Victoire. From that moment on she always had her nose stuck in a book with an expression that seemed to say: "I'm the only one in this house who has other things on her mind than stuffing her face with food."

Throughout her life she affected to despise material pleasures, especially the culinary arts. But was it really an affectation? All began probably by a banal adolescent revolt that gradually took root in reality.

Every Thursday at ten o'clock, in the study where Jeanne did her homework, Victoire persisted in bringing her a cup of vanilla-flavored chocolate that she never drank. One day, without looking up from her exercise books and manuals, she let out:

"I want to go to Versailles."

Versailles was the name of the boarding school recently opened in Basse-Terre by the Sisters of Saint-Joseph-de-Cluny.

"*Vèsaye?*" Victoire asked her in dismay. "*Pouki sa?*"

Why? Jeanne did not take the trouble to open her mouth, since the answer was written all over her face: uncommunicative, evasive, stony, and stubborn. Basse-Terre was situated at the other end of the island. She wanted to get away from the Walberg household, from this circle of bourgeois white Creoles who despised her on account of her color and whom she despised on account of their lack of education. Above all, she wanted to get away from her mother, a dull-witted vassal who obliged her to live in their midst. If at that instant Victoire had burst into tears, thus revealing the extent of her chagrin, perhaps the rest of their lives would have been different. But as usual her oblique eyes showed no feelings. She laid the tray on the desk and without a word went out into the corridor. It was there, severely shaken, that she leaned up against the wall to stop herself from fainting. All day long, her heart bled. She did not confide her agony to Anne-Marie, who was deciphering a page of *Faust* by Gounod in her room while gobbling cashew nuts from La Désirade. She waited for nightfall to open her heart to Boniface, lying next to her in the Regency room. He was the only one who would consent to this extraordinary expense. Unhappy about having to part with his money, he pulled a face. Won't Jeanne ever tire of studying? Wasn't she content with what she knew already? The Versailles boarding school had an undeniable reputation. "The school places great care on education," writes a report by the public education authorities. "We have found it to be sound, clean, with an abundance of healthy food."

This, no doubt, explained the high cost of its tuition and accommodation. Disbursing such a sum was out of the question. At the same time Boniface was always anxious to please his Victoire. He hit on the idea of a compromise. Jeanne would have to sit for a competitive examination and win one of the school's scholarships to finance her studies.

Monsieur Roumegoux's services were once again called upon. Since Boniface Jr. had turned out to be a dunce and managed to keep the store's books as best he could, and Valérie-Anne, despite her mother's hesitations, had been entrusted to a private institution, the family no longer had need of his tuition. Anne-Marie begged him to come back. Every day he turned up at the rue de Nassau to give Jeanne her algebra and geometry lessons (her weak points), teach her a little English—he had lived in Roseau in Dominica—and discuss literature, for despite her young age she showed a very sound judgment. For instance, she adored the short stories by Guy de Maupassant. Monsieur Roumegoux introduced her to the writer he admired above all: Baudelaire. He gave her this quotation from *Les Paradis artificiels* to reflect upon: "Common sense tells us that earthly matters have very little relevance and that true reality can be found only in dreams."

On May 19, 1906, Jeanne was the first black girl to pass the examination with the mention "Excellent," which opened the doors to the Versailles boarding school.

IN ORDER TO symbolize the farewell she was making to a certain way of life, she insisted on traveling alone to Basse-Terre. No chaperone, if you please. Since Victoire was afraid of her traveling on the steamship *Hirondelle,* which had overturned several times, she insisted she take the more reliable diligence over land, which took seven hours to travel between La Pointe and Basse-Terre, following the Windward Coast via Capesterre. For an entire week, she silently cross-stitched Jeanne's initials, JQ, on a trousseau generously provided by the Walbergs: six single sheets, twelve terry towels, and twenty-four cotton panties. The nuns didn't do things by halves. She was dying to talk to Jeanne, but didn't know how to go about it. It was from that moment on, I believe, that she began to fear her daughter's secretive and impenetrable character. What lay behind this face, so pretty, yet so cold?

The morning of Jeanne's departure, Victoire secured her daughter's two heavy wicker baskets on her head and accompanied her as far as the chamber of commerce, where the diligence began its journey.

I can see them now.

How different were the circumstances of this departure from the one in Marie-Galante sixteen years earlier, when the mother was trying to protect the daughter. This time it was the daughter fleeing the mother. Jeanne is walking in front, dressed in the elegant Scotch plaid uniform that the nuns demanded—pleated skirt flapping around her ankles, blouse buttoned up to the neck, patent leather pumps with a low heel, and a smart white Panama hat. She is tall, slender, and aloof. Something in her expression puts a stop to the racy jokes by the ragamuffins who are already idling in the streets. Hard on her heels, the mother with her headtie, heavily loaded, dressed in her shapeless dress with a leafy pattern, looking like a servant. The moment has come to climb into the diligence. The daughter brushes her mother's cheek with a cold kiss and hurriedly climbs into the vehicle. A few minutes later, the carriage lurches off with a creaking punctuated by the coachman's shout: "Forward!" The mother stands motionless, head lowered, at the edge of the sidewalk. She doesn't see her daughter making a farewell gesture to her at the carriage door. She senses she is losing her and wonders what caused such a separation. What is she guilty of? What mistakes has she made? She gave her the best schooling and best education possible. The weapons she used, questionable, despicable perhaps, were the only ones within her reach. Was that why her child was rejecting her?

She retraces her footsteps. All around her the streets are bustling with activity, filled with the pleasant smell from the droppings of the horse-drawn carriages. Servants are on their way to market.

"*Corossol doudou,*" shouts a fruit seller sitting at the crossroads.

In the dining room, Anne-Marie, bursting out of her orange dressing gown, is savoring her cup of chocolate and array of cassava breads.

"*I pati?*" she asks.

Yes, she's gone. All morning long, Victoire is plunged sadly in the preparation of a curried skate *colombo*.

I have never seen Anne-Marie with my own two eyes, although the picture of this obese musician has constantly haunted my imagination. I have collected the bizarre rumors that circulated about her. At the end of her life, almost destitute as a result of her son's dissolute existence, she holed herself up in her room on the second floor of the house on the rue de Nassau, surviving thanks to the goodness of her daughter. All that remained were a few pieces of rich-looking furniture, flotsam from her life of splendor. She could no longer get downstairs. Folds of fat prevented her from wedging her viola under her chin. Her pudgy fingers could no longer handle her bow. She apparently owned an old phonograph and listened to operas from morning to night while tirelessly nibbling on *rahat-loukoum*, stuffed dates, *grabyo koko*, grilled peanuts, and candies such as *douslets* and *sik a koko têt roz*.

ELEVEN

From the time Jeanne left for Versailles, Victoire's life took on a more somber coloring. It was not just the gray routine of life, even grayer since the aborted dream of Martinique. It was the black of frustration and suffering that was slowly overwhelming her. She had trouble getting over her daughter's bitterness and had difficulty understanding it. She plunged herself in her cooking while her talent reached a perfection of fantasy and inventiveness, even though the Walbergs were the only ones to profit from it since they no longer entertained at home. She knew only too well that Jeanne was ashamed of her. Consequently, against Anne-Marie's advice, she refused to go and visit Jeanne in Basse-Terre. She could see herself in the visitor's room, in the covered playground with her daughter under the gaze of the nuns in cornets. She would stick out like a sore thumb from the other parents, educated and well dressed white Creoles and mulattoes. How they would all look her up and down! How they would snigger behind her back! As a result, for one entire school year, mother and daughter communicated solely through the letters that Jeanne sent to La Pointe once a month and that Anne-Marie read out loud:

My dear mother,

My dear godmother,

Dear Monsieur Walberg,

I am very well except for a cough that starts especially in the evening because the air that blows down from the mountain is cool, almost cold. I had to buy two woolens chez Rivier. Yesterday the nuns took us to mass for the month of Mary at the Carmel church. It was five o'clock in the afternoon and not a soul in the streets. Every house had its shutters lowered. Apparently that's how they live in Basse-Terre: behind closed shutters.

With love and affection.

ALL THE WHILE dreading the long school holidays, Victoire drew the little strength she possessed in the hope they would reunite her with her daughter. Alas! In June a letter informed her that Jeanne would not take her holidays until September. She had been chosen by the nuns to teach remedial French classes in July and August, an honor of distinction for a first-year pupil and a tribute to her intelligence.

In her chagrin, Victoire transferred her little treats onto Valérie-Anne. She was in dire need of them, the poor girl, for she was growing up skinny and red-haired, her brother's punching bag, ignored by mother and father alike. The affection that bonded Victoire to Valérie-Anne must have outraged Jeanne and aroused in her a blind jealousy. On the subject of Valérie-Anne, Jeanne, who was always restrained in her words, lost all proportion and could go on for hours:

"A real bitch. Ever since the cradle. A flirt into the bargain. A nymphomaniac, I bet. She was always jealous of me, trying to appropriate what belonged to me. She would walk into my room without knocking and take my things."

She accused her of all the sins of Israel. Her former protégée, according to her, had transformed herself into a rival.

Around the end of the year, Boniface bought an automobile, an event worth noting. Up till then he had been terrified of the first internal combustion engines. And then he had a craze for horses and mounted himself a handsome chestnut, an American Thoroughbred, which he raced occasionally at Dugazon. But one has to keep up with the times. He decided on a gleaming six-cylinder Cleveland, which he struggled to learn to drive, whose headlamps were as round as a pair of wide-open eyes. You should have seen him: the type of goggles that Charles Lindbergh later wore perched on his nose and wrapped in a flowing muffler as seen in *Once Upon a Time in the West*. This purchase of an automobile was followed by another one, the acquisition of a change-of-air house in Vernou in the hills of La Lézarde.

The place was becoming fashionable and was soon to be the favorite spot of the bourgeois classes from La Pointe. A deputy governor of the colony, who in a single day had seen four of his eight children carried off by a fever, had built a house there for the months of July to October, when the climate in town was so deleterious. The idea of a change-of-air house in Vernou was odd at the time because for those who lived on Grande Terre, the actual island of Guadeloupe, as it was called, appeared to be a sinister back of beyond. Few of the inhabitants of La Pointe had ever ventured as far as Basse-Terre, capital of the island as decreed by the colonial authorities. As for the river Salée, it could now be crossed without mishap. After years of I don't know how many drownings and accidents, a pontoon bridge called the Union Bridge had replaced the former Gabarre Bridge.

The Walbergs' change-of-air house was magnificent. It stood out from the rest by one remarkable detail: an outside spiral metal staircase. The house was situated to the left of the present Route de la Traversée, next to the small factory called Vernou Jalousy. Once Boniface Sr. had been buried, to prevent it from falling into the hands of her son, Anne-Marie sold it to her cousins the Desmarais, who in turn sold it to a mulatto magistrate. Today it is almost a ruin, squatted for years by a colony of reddened-lock Rastas who grow ganja in the immense garden where once flourished orchids, trumpet flowers, and the proud canna lily.

Boniface drove Anne-Marie, Victoire, and Valérie-Anne there in early July. It was a genuine expedition. The servants left the day before by diligence. As early as five o'clock in the morning they loaded the car with trunks of linen and hampers brimming with victuals. Victoire held the provisions on her lap. At that time the roads were narrow ribbons made slippery by the slightest rain. Once they had left Petit Bourg, under Boniface's inexperienced hands the Cleveland slid, skidded, and jolted, getting bogged down along the winding track that crossed the forest.

To the right and left the ebony, silk cotton, gum and manjack trees, every variety of mahogany and acoma, parasitized by hundreds of creepers, epiphytes, and wild pineapples, jostled one another amid a riot of light to dark green. From the undergrowth came the harsh caws of the numerous parrots that used to be a common sight on the island, and the trills of the hummingbirds. Sheets of boiling or icy water fell from invisible heights with a deafening roar and splashed onto the track, making it even more impracticable.

Anne-Marie was snoring. She had not appreciated the purchase of this change-of-air house. Not only because she made a point of honor to disapprove of all of Boniface's decisions, but above all, as we have already said, because she loathed the countryside. For her, it was all mosquitoes, mabouya geckos, and crazy ants. Victoire, on the other hand, somewhat to her surprise, took a liking to Vernou; it was as if you had been transported to another planet, so different from the implacable glare of Marie-Galante. All day long, a metallic gray sky sat low on this mass of green. The rain never tired of falling. Not the raging, torrential rain like the frequent thundershowers in La Pointe. But a penetrating drizzle. A rain that never let up.

After lunch, while Anne-Marie was taking her siesta, Victoire would leave for a walk with Valérie-Anne. They would delve under the canopy of trees, winding along twisting paths through the forest and the giant tree ferns. The child was a good walker. They often walked as far as the chapel at Fontarabie. The modest wooden edifice would loom up as white as a ghost between the mossy trunks. Victoire and Valérie-Anne never met anyone there. Yet the invisible supplicants who had preceded them had lit candles and piled bunches of heliconia, lobster claw, and torch ginger flowers at the feet of the plaster saints. Sometimes, when it wasn't raining too hard, Victoire would take Valérie-Anne to swim in the pool at Prise d'Eau that was crossed by a rudimentary bridge. Oxen came down to drink there. Neighboring kids came to splash around. Women filled buckets they perched on their heads and men fished for crayfish. The individuals of both sexes, even the children, looked like scarecrows: in rags, a muddy skin, riddled with scurvy and kwashiorkor. While the little girl plunged into the icy water in panties and blouse, Victoire took off her shoes and dabbled her feet. She too would have liked to go for a swim. But the thought of baring her white body seemed shockingly indecent to her. So she sat there thinking of Jeanne, torturing herself over and over. She had wanted a better life for her daughter than one of abject poverty. She had wanted to give her a future and help her climb the social ladder. She now blamed herself for lacking audacity. There was the example of this woman nicknamed Mama Accra who was making a small fortune selling very ordinary cod fritters to sailors and dock workers. She was the talk of La Pointe.

Dusk and its sudden darkness brought them back to Vernou.

When they arrived, Maby and Délia had already set candles in the candlestick holders and placed earthenware pots in which lemongrass was burning to drive away the mosquitoes. Anne-Marie was sight-reading some Bach in her room. Valérie-Anne huddled up against Victoire in fright. A wall had closed in around the house, thick and impenetrable. Oh God! What was that on the branch of the ylang-ylang tree? What was that galloping along the road? Was it Man Ibè's three-legged horse? It sounded just like it: clippity-clop, clippity-clop. It was hardly more reassuring inside. The flickering from the candles drew a carnival of grinning faces on the walls. The childless mother cuddled in her arms the motherless child, and other tales welled up in her heart as she remembered the nights with Caldonia:

Sé té an madamm ki te ni an ti bolòm . . .

Ah, if only she had nestled her child against her breast like this! If only she had played her lullabies on the guitar! The truth was that Jeanne had always intimidated her. Even as a baby in her cradle gorged with milk, Jeanne would raise her little head and look at her with gleaming eyes. She was her daddy's daughter. Not hers. She belonged to that world of audacity, ambition, moral strength, and intelligence. Not hers: the one where the servants know only how to say Yes, Master.

At the end of July, the two Bonifaces arrived and brought a change of routine. They could no longer bear the oven that La Pointe had become. The end of the dry season had been terrible. As a result of the heat, fires had devastated the outlying districts and burnt two or three large families to a cinder. In a single night seventeen children had perished. The health services now feared another outbreak of yellow fever. Consequently, those who had the means fled to take refuge in the vicinity of Saint-Claude because of its altitude and the proximity to the Camp Jacob hospital. The actual truth was that Boniface Sr. found he had been deprived of his beloved Victoire far too long. As for Boniface Jr., he had had enough of his daily trips to the store on the Lardenoy wharf. Once he was in the constant company of his mother, however, he regretted his decision.

Four weeks later, in early September, it was Jeanne's turn to arrive from Basse-Terre after a ten-hour carriage drive to Petit-Bourg. There she had completed her journey in an ox cart. The driver succumbed under the weight of a trunk whose contents of books she proudly displayed on the shelves of a *deux corps* bookcase. Guy de Maupassant. Stendhal. Balzac. Flaubert. Baudelaire. She showed little emotion on seeing her mother, whom she hadn't embraced for over a year, and she did not scold her for never visiting her at the boarding school. On this point, they understood each other without saying a word. However, at dinner—an extravaganza of conch and crab invented by Victoire in her honor—Jeanne proved she had a soft spot to anyone who doubted it. She had spent all the money she had earned from her remedial courses to buy a gold choker from Luigi Venutolo, the finest jeweler in La Pointe, which she clasped around her mother's neck. It was the first piece of jewelry that Vic-

toire possessed, except for a pair of Creole earrings and a chain, neither of which had much value, a gift from Anne-Marie or Boniface.
It brought tears to Victoire's eyes. Yet all she could do was whisper
a thank-you with head lowered:

"Mèsi!"

Then mother and daughter embraced awkwardly. After that,
Jeanne ripped at her mother's heart by refusing to taste her dish.
She insisted she was not hungry, was utterly exhausted, and with-
drew very early to the room she had been allocated.

Jeanne was never to set foot in Vernou again. Not that she did
not like the area. The first thing she did when she decided to build
a change-of-air house with my father was to choose a spot at Sarcelles, only a few miles from Vernou in the district of Petit-Bourg. It
was because during this stay she accumulated a store of bad memories. She found the situation utterly unbearable. Although large,
the house did not have the arrangements or configuration of the
one on the rue de Nassau. All the rooms were on the same level
with a wraparound veranda and no attic. Maby and Délia slept in
a small cabin at the bottom of the garden. Amid this promiscuity, together with the casualness of the holidays, the masks were
off. Jeanne could not bear seeing Victoire and Boniface go into the
same bedroom holding a candle. The four-poster bed of locustwood
where they slept seen through the half-open door made her vomit.
At night she listened for every creak in the wood. Her frenzied mind
mistook the groan of the wind for her mother's moans of pleasure,
and in the morning she would stare at her in disgust. She was no
different than a courtesan, a woman who sold her body, except that
those Italian women were usually excellent poets, whereas Victoire
couldn't even read. Her mood translated into her refusal to feed
herself, which perhaps today we would call anorexia or something
similar. At mealtimes she would ostentatiously push her plate away
after one or two mouthfuls and claim that the delicious smells of
basil, ginger, and saffron that emerged from the kitchen made her
feel sick. She disliked Valérie-Anne's pranks. She could not stand

Anne-Marie's and Victoire's musical sessions. Anne-Marie's viola got on her nerves and the faltering chords of her mother's guitar and recorder exasperated her.

Plus Boniface Jr.'s advances.

Well hung like his father, but rougher and more enterprising, he was always touching her, groping her breasts and buttocks. One morning he managed to enter her room, where she was reading *La Chartreuse de Parme* in bed. He greedily planted a kiss on her mouth while his hand undid his fly. What a pity for my story he did not take her by force! Unfortunately, nothing serious happened. She fought him off. They remained staring at each other, both panting with desire. But Jeanne would have died rather than admit it.

Another time she went with her mother and Valérie-Anne to Prise d'Eau. Boniface Jr. caught up with them unawares, and since the weather was fine he went for a swim. At the time the mere idea of nudity was improper. The beauty of this athlete's body parading his assets that were difficult to conceal aroused in Jeanne an emotion she felt to be shameful. In a rage, she returned home to Vernou alone.

Thereupon, Jeanne imagined that in order to humiliate her Anne-Marie was encouraging her son. This seems unlikely given the little interest she showed in her son. In fact, she only spoke to him when they were bridge partners. Jeanne, however, felt really humiliated—or quite simply jealous—when looking out of her bedroom window in the predawn she saw Boniface Jr. creep out of the maid's quarters. He was sleeping with one of them, but which one? Délia was at least ten years older than he was and mother of a multitude of children. Maby was just a kid. In his eyes, therefore, she was nothing but black meat he could take for pleasure as he wished. Not an ounce of feeling in his propositions. Moreover, she was convinced a white man could never love a black woman. Only lust and concupiscence could exist between them.

In fact, the holidays ended unpleasantly for everyone. It was the very height of the rainy season. That year there were no hurricanes

or gales, but the rain intensified. Torrents of water poured monoto-
nously from the sky. The gutters overflowed. The garden was transformed into a muddy lake. The rain put an end to the walks through
the forest or swimming at Prise d'Eau. They would drink grogs with
heavy doses of Féneteau *les grappes blanches* rum. As a distraction,
relatively speaking, on Sundays, braving the bad weather, the family would drive down to the church in Petit-Bourg where Boniface
had negotiated the hire of a pew in the center aisle. The Walbergs
huddled together on the bench under the inquisitive looks of the
natives: Anne-Marie and the two Bonifaces displaying their ostentatious devotion as notables and declaiming in a loud voice the words
in Latin; Valérie-Anne, bored to death; Victoire, crushed by the
silent hostility of her daughter, barely containing her tears; Jeanne
having no time for the Confiteor, the Agnus Dei, or the Sanctus, but
beating her breast instead and repeating:

"I hate them! I hate them!"

The only distraction.

Because they kept on meeting them in front of the church, before or after mass, the Walbergs discovered they were related to
the Rueil-Bonfils, owners of the Roujol factory on the outskirts of
Petit-Bourg. This factory is now defunct. When I was a child it still
existed but already looked a ruin. I often cycled over there. I can
remember its blackened, dilapidated silhouette, a wreck washed up
in the midst of an ocean of cane fields.

One Sunday, the Rueil-Bonfils invited the Walbergs for lunch in
their opulent house beside the factory, and it soon became a ritual.
The Rueil-Bonfils tribe could easily have figured in a French sit-
com: the mustached grandfather in a wheelchair; the grandmother,
hale and hearty, also with a mustache; an aunt, an old maid, with
dangling ringlets held in place by a black velvet ribbon; a libidinous
uncle, mentally handicapped, who exposed himself to little boys;
the dignified father; the mother, a platinum blonde; a dozen children, including a little blind girl who played the piano four-handed
with her twin brother. They would all sit down together after mass.

As soon as Victoire arrived, she would docilely tie on an apron and join the other servants around the charcoal burners in the kitchen. Meanwhile, Jeanne would go and sit with the visitors in the drawing room or in the garden, weather permitting. With her black skin, she was looked upon as a curiosity by the Rueil-Bonfils, who practically blamed the Walbergs for treating her as an equal. She had to confront a barrage of questions that were a mixture of paternalism, hypocrisy, and racism.

So she was at boarding school at Versailles! And studying for her elementary school certificate?

No! Studying for the *superior* school certificate!

And she studied Latin as well?

Yes, she knew a little Latin.

So she was counting on becoming an elementary school teacher? What a wonderful profession!

Good Lord, the Negroes have come a long way since they arrived from Africa, beasts of burden under the whip! We may very well ask ourselves, however, whether they have really evolved. Still as lazy, depraved, and calculating. On this subject, the Rueil-Bonfils kept reeling off a never-ending stock of stories about the behavior of their factory workers.

One day, Félicité, who liked to think she knew a thing or two about literature, with a spiteful smile offered Jeanne a short novel by Anaïs Ségalas, her idol, called *Tales of the Antilles: The Forest of La Soufrière*. Since by an amusing coincidence I had been awarded the Anaïs Ségalas Prize by the Académie Française for one of my books, *Tree of Life*, I made inquiries about this writer and discovered she was a Creole from Saint-Domingue who in her time had enjoyed a certain reputation. I even read her book reedited by *L'Harmattan*. It's a worthless pack of racist ideas of that time, curiously combined with an abolitionist rehash. Here is an extract: "Jupiter must have been about thirty; he was a Negro of African race of the finest black or rather the ugliest. He was of average height, strong and energetic. Like all Negroes his feet were deformed and extended behind and in front of his shinbone. His hair was woolly. The bottom of his face stretched out like a muzzle."

Did Félicité intend to hurt Jeanne, whose intelligence we would have thought was above such stupidity? In any case, she hit her mark and my mother suffered enormously. In fact, she never stopped suffering. At mealtimes, when Victoire served up culinary delights of her invention, a capon with breadnuts, for example, she received an ovation and a heap of praise that implied she at least knew her place. Not like some people. Jeanne never stopped asking herself whether she ought not to make a scene, stand up, and leave. I do believe that what consequently came to be known as her "impossible nature" was born from having suffered her humiliation in silence out of respect for her mother. The worst of it all, however, was that Aymeric Rueil-Bonfils was competing with Boniface Jr. He insisted on openly courting her, encouraged by the entire family, according to him. She in fact sensed that the family would have applauded if she had been generous with her favors, just as Victoire had been generous with Boniface, thus regaining her true vocation.

All this suddenly came to an end.

One day out of the blue, Anne-Marie declared she didn't like Félicité Rueil-Bonfils, who knew nothing about music. In fact, all she talked about were her books and her simple or double flowering gardenias. Valérie-Anne whimpered because the children of her own age poked fun at her pilosity and called her Red Head. Since Boniface Jr. mistakenly imagined that Jeanne preferred Aymeric, he decided Aymeric was one hell of a joker. Aymeric boasted that his mare Torride always came first at the races and won him sums obviously multiplied by ten. Only Boniface Sr. could possibly like the company of Amédée Sr. Knowing he was in desperate straits, riddled with debts and vainly seeking a buyer for the factory, reassured him in his conviction that trade was a better choice than sugar.

Finally, the loathsome holidays drew to an end. The Walbergs left for La Pointe. Jeanne for Versailles. This time she did exactly as she pleased and chose the steamer that only took six and a half hours, stopping at Sainte-Rose, Deshaies, and Pointe-Noire.

For two years Victoire didn't visit her. Only their letters provided a semblance of communication between them. During those years Jeanne worked herself to death and passed her school certificate with the grade "Very Good" plus "Congratulations from the Jury," which opened the doors to the teaching profession. But that wasn't enough for her. In a long, detailed epistle she explained that she would have to continue studying at Versailles for another year. This long separation without the holidays in Vernou, since Jeanne regularly taught remedial classes during the long vacation, was extremely damaging for the relations between mother and daughter. Victoire, feeling abandoned, withdrew further into herself, cooking to excess. At that time when refrigeration did not exist, you couldn't keep food for more than a day or two. Délia and Maby distributed the leftovers to the families of the needy *maléré*, carefully selected for their good behavior and their devotion to God. Boniface, so particular about waste, did not protest. Everything his Victoire did was right. She drew even closer to Anne-Marie, who had no need for an explanation, since she could read her like an open book, and thus played certain pieces especially for her. The afternoon sessions therefore changed. Victoire no longer fiddled on her guitar or practiced on her flute. With eyes closed, sitting in her rocking chair, she listened. At times, painful sighs welled up in her breast and tears rolled down her cheeks. Yet Anne-Marie never intervened with questions or words of consolation. She left it up to the music to do its work.

TWELVE

The newspaper *Le Nouvelliste* celebrated Jeanne's success at passing her final, superior school diploma with a vibrant article headline "Onward, Negress! Forge ahead!"

Beneath the headline was a photo, alas not a very attractive one. My mother, as lovely as she was, never was photogenic. In front of the lens, she would tense up, become stressed, and in the end look like a hunted animal. In addition, the newspaper listed with satisfaction the names of the four young black girls, including her, who had received their final diploma. They were the first of their race. The pictures of these pioneers appeared in *Femmes en devenir*, a journal we might label as feminist, as well as in the monthly magazine *La Guadeloupe de demain*. Ever since Marie de la Redemption, the Mother Superior of the convent school at Versailles, had declared in *Diocèses de France* that in all her career she had never come across such a brilliant mind, from one day to the next Jeanne became a kind of star, public opinion crediting her with a superior intelligence. In reality, the Mother Superior and her pupil had never got on together, the former constantly reproaching the latter for her arrogance, susceptibility, and impertinence. The latter reproaching the former for her racism. Jeanne did not keep happy memories of

Versailles. I admire her courage and determination to spend three years there. Three years of her youth when she could have been laughing, dancing, and flirting. In light of the Walbergs' recommendation, the convent, which admitted only legitimate children, made an exception for Jeanne, whereas the other pupils had never tolerated her and at the slightest opportunity reminded her who she was.

Perhaps out of respect for Victoire, Anne-Marie wanted Jeanne to celebrate her success at rue de Nassau. They would invite Monsieur Roumegoux and Father Moulinet, who taught the children catechism and gave Jeanne her first communion. Jeanne refused, with the excuse that she was obliged to attend a teaching course in Basse-Terre. I don't know whether it is possible to imagine exactly how Victoire felt as she contemplated the picture of her daughter in the newspapers. Even if she could not read the accompanying articles brimming with praise, her heart was no doubt bursting with pride. What a revenge she had taken on Dernier! Without his help, she had prized open heavily padlocked doors for her daughter. Without his help, she was offering her a radiant future. I believe, however, that these feelings were mixed with a great deal of sadness. She was fully aware that this success had been paid for dearly, too dearly, acquired at the price of too much humiliation. She was making her child inaccessible, locked in a prison where the air was rarefied. My mother was of the same opinion. I constantly heard her exclaim in a tone of voice that was unmistakably ambiguous: "My mother could neither read nor write, but without her I wouldn't be where I am today."

Where was she? Those who had eyes understood full well that she did not see herself in paradise.

In October, she was assigned her first teaching position. Then as now, it was the custom to assign beginners to the most thankless schools. But her results were so exceptional that instead of sending her off to La Désirade, Terre-de-Haut in Les Saintes, or some other godforsaken hole, the Ministry of Education appointed her to Le

Moule, the second largest town on the island, with more inhabitants than Basse-Terre.

I don't know what the monthly salary of a young female elementary school teacher was in 1909, but I do know it was one-fifth below that of a man's. Such as it was, it allowed her no doubt to support her mother. Jeanne hastened to ask Victoire to come and live with her. Ill-informed and bad-mouthing are those who claim that once she had assured her daughter's education, Victoire rushed to drop the Walbergs like a crab drops its claw, as the saying goes. For two months she turned a deaf ear to her daughter's pleas. To the point that in November, Jeanne, stung to the quick, had to come and fetch her herself in La Pointe.

What was Victoire afraid of? Did she think this invitation was dictated by propriety? Couldn't she resign herself to leave Boniface and especially Anne-Marie?

We do not know the details of the separation and if it really was surrounded in drama. We do know, however, that at six thirty one morning, when it was raining cats and dogs, Jeanne and Victoire climbed aboard a carriage that in four hours drove them to Le Moule. Throughout the journey they did not say a word to each other, each locked in her gloomy thoughts. On arrival, Jeanne hired the services of a street porter who wheeled her mother's trunk through the streets on a barrow.

"Le Moule has a melancholy air about it," someone wrote at the time, "and its wide streets are empty. A devastating fire has swept through the town! The town is dead, the port abandoned, the only edifice standing, the church, the only walk, the graveyard." The town was not only melancholy. It was overpopulated and wretched. Although in this sugar-producing region the factories at Zevallos, Gardel, and Blanchet procured a seasonal employment for the workers from the former plantations, they did not provide any *kaz-nèg*, in other words any lodging. The workers were forced to crowd into an ever-growing number of shacks surrounding the center of town. Jeanne had rented a two-room cabin, tiny but prettily painted in light gray with green persienne shutters, just two steps from the rue Saint-Jean, a flourishing neighborhood lined with the shops and warehouses of the white Creole merchants. The interior was sparingly furnished, for she had refused the slightest gift from Anne-Marie, whose house on the rue de Nassau was crammed with furniture: low tables, high tables, square or oval, chairs, sleigh beds, canopy beds, four-poster beds, all locked away in the attic. She would have liked Victoire to share her bed—a so-called bed *à boules*, padded with two mattresses, a bolster, and two pillows—in which she saw a symbol of her new station. But Victoire remained intransigent. A straw mattress thrown on the floor would be quite sufficient for her. Up at four in the morning, they would walk to mass, Victoire trotting behind as she always did. Back home, they would drink their coffee in silence. Scalding hot, black, and heaped with sugar. Then Jeanne would leave for the elementary school for girls, which used to be where the present technical lycée stands. Left on her own, Victoire had plenty to do. She would dust the furniture, air the straw mattress, beat the others, sweep the floor, scrub it three times a week, wash her daughter's clothes, whiten and starch them, then iron them. Since she was a real workaholic, the housework was finished around eleven. Her day was then over. Since Jeanne ate nothing or very little, there was no cooking to be done. I wonder what it meant for Victoire never to set foot in the kitchen. Never to match savors and colors. Never to breathe in the smell of spices. No longer to be God.

Such a situation is comparable to that of a writer who, due to circumstances beyond her control, is kept from her computer. What torture! How does she fight that terrible feeling of uselessness that assails her?

At eleven thirty Jeanne would return home from school, perspiring despite the parasol she held over her head, for Le Moule is a stifling town. Hot waves of feverish gusts would blow in from the ocean. Mother and daughter, without a word, would lunch off a salad. Jeanne would leave for school again. At first, during her absence, Victoire did not get out of the house and stayed cooped up in the cramped interior. Then around four in the afternoon she got into the habit of walking as far as the ocean, the Atlantic on this side of Guadeloupe, raging, boiling, and roaring. It was bordered by a promenade, a sort of *malecòn*, planted with thatch palms. Little towns, like little countries, don't like strangers, those who come from God knows where. They sniff them with distrust, for danger lurks in the folds of their clothes. The inhabitants of Le Moule would watch Victoire. "The new schoolmistress's mother" boded no good. She would walk, machinelike, absorbed in her thoughts. Sometimes she would sit on a bench, savoring the sea breeze. Jeanne finished school at five in the afternoon. She would return home, her parasol under her arm, preceded by a pupil proud to be carrying the exercise books. In the light of an oil lamp she sat engrossed in her corrections, while Victoire remained outside on a bench. Women selling grilled peanuts and *topinambos* set up shop not far from her on the sidewalk, but did not engage in conversation with the stranger. The night gradually closed in around her motionless figure, the racket of the insects grew louder, and the great voice of the ocean intensified into a howling roar.

I interviewed Léonie X, who has lived all her life in the anchorage district and as a child used to see Victoire. "She scared me," she confided in me. "All alone in the dark. Maman convinced me she was *gagé*, had made a pact with the devil to leave her skin on the side of the road and turn herself into a dog. Sometimes she lit a pipe and it glowed like a big eye."

One Sunday in December, an event somewhat out of the ordinary came to trouble the morning routine. The sound of a Cleveland automobile roaring past the church, in front of which the faithful out of high mass were still chattering, drew a crowd of neighbors. Boniface, with aviator goggles and muffler, stepped out of the car while the neighbors in their curiosity rushed out onto their doorsteps. He shyly planted his lips on Victoire's forehead and asked how she was.

"Sa ou fè?"
"An bien mèsi."

He had brought a gift: a gramophone, a highly sophisticated English make that had cost him a fortune, together with a box of records. Since he had been guided by whatever took his fancy, his choice was somewhat disparate. It included beguines, Christmas carols, and patriotic hymns such as "The Song of Departure." Nevertheless, he had not forgotten Anne-Marie's favorite work, Bach's Concerto for Two Violins, or an assortment of opera excerpts. Thus, failing her cooking, Victoire rediscovered the joy of music and the melodies from *Carmen:*

> *L'amour est enfant de Bohême*
> *Il n'a jamais jamais connu de loi*

Boniface's visit lasted exactly thirty minutes. As soon as he had downed a glass of *shrubb* prepared by Victoire since it was Christmas, he asked to be excused because of the long drive back to La Pointe. In actual fact it was too painful for him to be near his beloved Victoire and not take her in his arms. Above all, it was especially difficult to put up with Jeanne's gaze as she sat in a corner stiff as a poker: a mixture of disapproval, contempt, and anger. Confronted with such a look, everything that had bound him to Victoire for so many years became dirty, sordid, and guilt-ridden. As I have already said, relations between Jeanne and Boniface had considerably deteriorated well before her departure for Versailles. Once the best of friends, on the rue de Nassau they no longer spoke to each other; Jeanne would merely offer her forehead for a kiss each morning before stiffly taking her place at the breakfast table. There had never been a declaration of war between them, but a chill that prevented any communication.

Boniface's visit was the cause of the first quarrel between Jeanne and Victoire. Quarrel, moreover, is not the right word. It implies a sharp exchange of words, even insults. In the case in point, it was rather a monologue on the part of Jeanne, who, without ever raising her voice, expressed her irritation with Victoire sitting mute and withdrawn. The reasons for her anger could be summed up by her concern about what the neighbors would say. What will the neighbors think, seeing this white Creole sweep into their house as if he owned it? How could they think of them as respectable women?

In fact this first "quarrel," which was to be followed by a few others for the same reason, set a pattern. Victoire never opened her mouth or defended herself. Each time, she remained mute, as if petrified by her daughter's words. Like many children, Jeanne was possessive and therefore unfair. She could not allow Victoire to have feelings of affection for anyone but herself. Certainly not for Anne-Marie, and even less for Boniface. Although Jeanne was never attached to the socialist ideas of the time and seemed to me totally apolitical, in her eyes these white Creoles had merely exploited Victoire. Mainly she tensed up thinking of Boniface, who had shamefully abused her body. She sincerely hoped that no pleasure or emotion had come out of their embraces. She could not understand how Victoire could like living on the rue de Nassau and consider it home, where absolutely nothing belonged to her, not even the Regency room that housed her miserable personal effects in a wooden trunk, not even the bed she slept on. She could not understand either why she had never tried out anything else besides being a servant at the Jovials or the Walbergs, or imagined another setting for her life.

Boniface never came back to Le Moule, although he constantly sent Victoire presents by the driver of the charabanc that soon replaced the diligence. Presents as ill-assorted as his choice of music: an alarm clock concealed in a Swiss chalet, a coffee grinder, some lavender water, and, most surprising of all, a dozen Cholet cloth tea towels.

THIRTEEN

L e Moule had no cultural life to speak of. The only events that
brought a little distraction were the religious festivals of Easter,
the Feast of the Assumption, and Christmas. In such a monotonous
existence, the round of visits to the club of Grands Nègres constituted an essential element.

Lest we forget, her job as an elementary school teacher, one of
the first black elementary school teachers, invested Jeanne with a
heavy responsibility. Despite her young age, she was now enrolled
in the embryo of the bourgeoisie. She therefore had to form alli-
ances with the members of this prestigious club.

The round of visits was made on Sundays.

On those afternoons, Jeanne dressed to the nines, dabbed herself
with perfume, then fastened around her neck the gold choker she
had bought with her first wages since everyone was sized up by her
collection of jewelry. She then slipped on her silk stockings and patent leather pumps. A little mascara around the eyebrows, a little lip-
stick, and some rouge on her cheeks. Then, flanked by her mother,
who had put on her best *golle* dress, she turned the key in the door,
opened her parasol, and set off. A list of personalities was engraved
in her head, for she couldn't afford to forget anybody, otherwise

she would have made formidable enemies for herself: Monsieur So-and-So, first black physician; Monsieur So-and-So, first black pharmacist; Monsieur W——, first lawyer; Monsieur X——, first magistrate; Monsieur Y——, first customs inspector; Monsieur Z——, first court bailiff, et cetera, et cetera, while most of the batch comprised the first black elementary school teachers.

In immaculate drawing rooms smelling of wax polish, not a grain of dust on the Honduras mahogany furniture, while guests savored the coconut sorbet to the grate of the ice cream maker operated by a servant in the yard, the conversation would turn to politics. Jean-Hégésippe Légitimus was no longer the sole leader. The quarrel was raging around Achille René-Boisneuf, his sworn enemy whose wit was legendary. Hadn't this hotheaded polemist called Légitimus a "ghost" because of his chronic absenteeism at the National Assembly in Paris as well as at the Conseil Général in Guadeloupe? Some people were accusing him of being a traitor, who had denounced the "politics of race," and never failed to include a dutiful speech on serving the Race like a priest serving God, and the example that should be given to their unfortunate brothers still plunged in the hell of ignorance.

The most formidable of the Grands Nègres in Le Moule were without doubt M. and Mme. Outremont Faustin, who lived in a charming upstairs-downstairs house on the square in front of the church. The house has miraculously resisted the onslaught of the demolition workers and still exists not far from the multimedia library. Outremont, a dermatologist with a degree from Toulouse University, was married to Emma Boisfer, who taught music at the Catholic school for girls, La Voie Droite. Emma did not gain her reputation because of her fourth certificate of merit for singing, but because of her brother Sylandre. Sylandre had studied at the National School of France Overseas and numbered among the colonial governors from the Antilles since he had been appointed to Oubangui-Chari. Numerous photos showed him in full uniform parading among scarred but smiling Africans. The Faustins were a handsome couple. Monsieur Faustin, built massively like Paul Robeson, also sang with a bass voice. Madame Faustin was slender and graceful. Jogging enthusiasts before jogging became fashionable, they covered several miles before dawn every morning. The first time Jeanne introduced herself, her heart was pounding wildly, since it was a well-known fact they were scathing in their comments and made and broke reputations. Like every other examination, however, she passed this one with flying colors. The Faustins never stopped singing her praises: a little cold perhaps, but remarkable from every point of view. As for the mother, however, their verdict was irrevocable: she was impossible.

I have to admit that Victoire in fact was a problem.

Sitting on the edge of her Hepplewhite chair, she didn't say a word throughout all the conversations because she was incapable of handling French, that weapon without which all the doors of civilization remain closed. At the time, however, thanks to lessons by Valérie-Anne, she managed to memorize a few phrases:

"I'm very well, thank you."

"And how about you?"

"God willing."

"May it please God."

Unfortunately, she was not gifted. She would overdo the pronunciation with the most comical of effects. Sometimes, she would quite simply muddle everything up. For example, to the question "How are you, Madame Quidal?" she would invariably reply "God willing," despite the exasperated reprimands of Jeanne, who would lecture her like a child before they went out.

Soon, at the initiative of the Faustins or at least with their collusion, the Grands Nègres of Le Moule nicknamed her Madame Godwilling. But matters did not rest there. A neighbor reported the shocking visit by Boniface Walberg and a blaze of gossip began, kindled by the wind of maliciousness. Hadn't she been his mistress? But her daughter was too black, much too black to be his child. Who was the father? As a result, they dug up the past in Marie-Galante to discover that under her hypocritically pious air, Victoire had been a first-rate *bòbò* and a man-eater. Before Boniface Walberg, she had been the mistress of a Dulieu-Beaufort who, after he had finished with her, passed her on to his cousin. Not surprising there was such a pig swill! Mulatto women were known to have the hots. Oddly, nobody thought of Dernier Argilius, since the hero was above all suspicion. This mockery and malicious gossip got back to the ears of Jeanne and Victoire. We don't know what the mother thought, always impassive and walled in silence. It is quite likely that she was not too affected since she was used to being excluded. But I know that the daughter was divided between distress and helpless rage.

It would have been easy enough to stop frequenting such a collection of snobs and bad-mouthers. But Jeanne was incapable of doing such a thing. For her this was Desirada, the promised island for the sailors of Christopher Columbus, reached after days of misadventures. For better or for worse she had to carve out a place for herself. So Sunday after Sunday she started all over again her stations of the cross.

It was then, for once, that God himself intervened.

The priest in Le Moule knew Reverend Father Moulinet from the church of Saint-Pierre and Saint-Paul in La Pointe. The latter knew all about Victoire's culinary gifts, which on Sundays he had often been invited to sample. He told his colleague of the treasure that Le Moule had in its breast. The priest in Le Moule concocted the idea therefore of asking Victoire to cook for his soup kitchen. A modest edifice built of corrugated iron and wooden planks, answering to the wonderful name of the Open Door, served a hundred or so meals every day to the *maléré* of Le Moule. Victoire did not accept the proposition without the approval of Jeanne, who hesitated for a long time. In the case in point, however, cooking amounted to honoring God, and she ended up approving.

From that moment on, Victoire was back at her kitchen range. As soon as her housework was done she set off for the Open Door, where she worked until three in the afternoon. A crowd of country women helped her, slicing onions, grinding garlic, fanning the fire, and doing the washing up. They were all scared of her, her whiteness, her unsmiling face and kept very quiet.

Given his paltry resources, the priest in Le Moule had nothing but root vegetables, pigs' snouts and tails, saltfish, and sometimes tripe at his disposal. Occasionally, charitable merchants made him a present of goods that were going to spoil, such as crates of cauliflower, carrots, and turnips. Victoire metamorphosed everything. It was something like the Transfiguration. In her hands, the fattest, toughest, and gristliest pieces of meat turned tasty and melted in the mouth. The *maléré* in their amazement, unused to such good fortune, surged in and the numbers swelled more than fifty percent.

No longer able to contain his gratitude, the priest in Le Moule extolled Victoire's merits in his sermon at high mass and called her a true Christian. He went so far as to invoke the wedding at Cana when Jesus changed the water into wine. Fully aware of the malicious gossip rumored about her, he made it known that it is possible to massacre the French language and have one's heart in the right place.

Did this quash the gossip and the mockery, I wonder?

This first year of teaching at Le Moule coming after years of humiliation at Versailles forged my mother's philosophy of life and dictated the education she gave to us, her children. The whites and mulattoes are our natural enemies. But as for the Negroes, oh the Negroes, big or small, their wickedness is immense. They are hurricanes and earthquakes that we must guard against. She convinced us that friendship does not exist. We have to live alone. Above the crowd. Finally, she convinced us of the vulnerability of women. According to her, the reason why the inhabitants of Le Moule hounded her mother and sullied her reputation was because she was nothing but a woman living alone with her daughter, without a man to protect either of them. Neither father nor husband. In order to navigate the ruts of life with a minimum of damage, you need the arm of a man. But not any man! Love was a mystification, a folly that could very well be fatal. You needed to arm your heart and carefully choose for a partner a man whose personal qualities put him above the others and who stood tall like a protecting tree.

A Grand Nègre, in fact! We always came back to them.

During the long vacation, teachers who were starting out met at the Lycée Carnot in La Pointe for training courses.

Ever since it had been founded in 1883 following the initiative of Alexandre Isaac, himself a mulatto, director of home affairs in the government of Guadeloupe, the Lycée Carnot was more than a simple secondary school. It was a breeding ground for the budding intelligentsia of color. Under the shadow of its massive mango trees in the recreation yard, all whom Guadeloupe would count as important personalities would pass along its balconies. Since it was also a boarding school, it could house the trainees. This enabled Jeanne to keep a promise she had made years ago: never to set foot again in the rue de Nassau.

But what was to be done with Victoire?

She couldn't force her to stay behind in Le Moule without her. With a heavy heart she had no other choice but to let her return to the Walbergs, in other words to Boniface's bed. Victoire had the tact not to show her joy at the prospect of moving back to the rue de Nassau. But the shine in her eyes, the coloring of her cheeks, and the way her entire person came back to life spoke for themselves. The day she bade farewell to the Open Door she cooked a banquet for almost two hundred *maléré*, and people still remember it today. The priest at Le Moule noted in his diary: "Today, June 22nd, Madame Victoire Quidal surpassed herself. It is the Almighty who has manifested Himself in her hands." They say that some of the *malérés* in their gratitude carried Victoire's and her daughter's trunks free of charge to the diligence. But that remains to be confirmed.

I don't know what gave Victoire the greatest happiness on the rue de Nassau. Being back with Boniface? Or with Anne-Marie? Or being back in her den, her domain, her kitchen range? The market women, who had somewhat neglected the place, set off back to her kitchen, and every morning there was an unloading of treasures. Victoire would weigh the red-eyed rabbits in their white fur, and sniff the tench and red snapper. Her fingers tapped away, pattering and pouring the salt, saffron, and cardamom, cutting, boning, and trimming.

She was also happy to be back in the afternoons resounding with melodies. I bet too she was happy to be back with Valérie-Anne and Boniface Jr. A sincere affection bonded her to these two, whom she had seen born and who oddly enough remained closer to her than her own daughter. They both called her Mamito, and Boniface Jr. confided in her the name of all his conquests. Since he detested his mother, he was grateful to Victoire for giving his father stability and a semblance of happiness.

True to her discretion and taught by her lesson at Le Moule, she in no way wanted to embarrass Jeanne by her visits to the Lycée Carnot. Consequently, although the rue de Nassau is just two steps from the rue Sadi Carnot, they were separated for almost three months. Anne-Marie's radical change of attitude toward her god-child dates from that moment on. She had taken the brunt of a good many refusals and humiliations without saying a word in the interest of not hurting Victoire. But this time Jeanne's behavior, betraying a reprehensible indifference with regard to a mother whose only thoughts were for her daughter, shocked her deeply. From that moment on, she became downright hostile, making increasingly scathing attacks every day on her selfishness and vanity. Victoire did not agree.

"A pa fòt aye!" she murmured.

"It's not her fault?" thundered Anne-Marie.

Victoire absolved Jeanne almost entirely, considering she was more to pity than to blame, torn as Jeanne was between her filial love, her ambition, her pride, her narcissism, and that terrible fear of the Other that she has passed on to all of us, her children.

Unquestionably the happiest of the entire household was Boniface. Every night was an enchantment. Every meal, a feast.

"You're spoiling me, you're spoiling me," he would repeat, and you never knew whether he was thinking of his nocturnal or diurnal pleasures.

In the evening he would no longer stay behind at the club or lose his money at an occasional party of whist. On leaving the store on the Lardenoy wharf he would stop by the Place de la Victoire to listen to the municipal concerts. It was strange because he had no taste for music and would often doze off in the middle of the most remarkable adagios. It was because he loved to be with Victoire and even Anne-Marie. The proximity of these two women, who had woven his days, made him appreciate those left for him to live. When the musicians put away their instruments, ever so slowly the three of them would return home, not yet three old bag of bones, but already largely worn out.

At the very start of the twentieth century, life began to change for women. They did not yet have any rights. But at least they were no longer confined between four walls. Admittedly, daily mass, monthly confession, communion, and the weekly calalu constituted the bulk of their schedule. Yet every afternoon Anne-Marie dared set off with Victoire for the Place de la Victoire. This square, laid out and planted with grass, had become the town's throbbing heart. Anne-Marie and Victoire always chose the same bench near the music kiosk. Never satisfied, Anne-Marie sharply criticized the musicians' performance, especially the first violins and the choice of program. One concert alone found favor with her: the one given by an orchestra from Martinique. It began with some beguines and mazurkas and finished with the overture to *The Grand Duchess of Gerolstein* by Offenbach. Such eclecticism delighted her. She vehemently repeated her theory that there is no such thing as "highbrow music" or "popular music." There is only *music*. The rest is a matter of taste, which is up to the true musician to satisfy. Ever since she was a girl, Anne-Marie had uttered opinions that were not to be contradicted. Neither Victoire nor Boniface was in a position to stand up to her. Moreover, they didn't even bother.

One afternoon, the trio saw Jeanne loom up. She was walking with a group so absorbed in conversation that they looked neither right nor left. Each member of the group wore a subtle type of habit: all had identical dark complexions, spectacles, hairdos, jewels and shoes. The way these young people moved, spoke, and laughed testified they were conscious of forming an elite, an example for the rest of the island. Victoire had eyes only for her child. She who was so awkward, common, and unattractive, how had she managed to create such a prodigy? She was touched by her daughter's expression, which seemed to say: "Look at me. I'm the prototype of a new generation. Be careful! Hands off! I am not for any Tom, Dick, and Harry!"

If she had been less blinded by Jeanne, Victoire would have noticed by her side a Negro fitted perfectly into a navy serge three-piece suit, wearing a soft felt fedora, who had just turned forty, in sharp contrast to his extremely young companions. His walk was characteristic: as stiff as a poker, with his head thrown backward. This was my father, Auguste Boucolon, whom Jeanne had just met. Principal of a school for boys on the rue Henri IV, he was so highly regarded by his superiors that they had put him in charge of the teachers' training courses. He was thinking, however, of leaving the teaching profession, since he had other ambitions in mind and had no intention of finishing his life as a civil servant. He had been so dazzled by Jeanne that she had made him speechless, something that seldom occurred. Jeanne, however, had not reciprocated. She found him *bodzè*, a bit of a dandy, somewhat common with his fine mustache. But she wasn't used to being desired or regarded as an irreplaceable precious object.

What nobody knows is that on that particular afternoon as she walked past the kiosk with her colleagues, Jeanne was perfectly aware of Victoire seated between her white Creole patrons. On the right, her mistress, elegantly dressed in a two-piece suit of georgette crepe, although a little too stout, wearing a gold choker, her complexion skillfully enhanced by her makeup. On her left, her boss, his suit a little too tight, he too somewhat potbellied, somewhat big-bottomed, a starched collar digging into his Adam's apple, with a jet-black mustache and a full head of hair that resisted the passing years. Victoire the servant, so much like a servant, held in her lap a parasol, a handbag, and a skipping rope belonging to Valérie-Anne, who was playing nearby. Go and kiss her? That would mean introducing her and the Walbergs to her friends. Jeanne guessed the thoughts that dared not be uttered and the remarks made behind her back. She imagined the conversation:

"How are you, Madame Quidal?"

"God willing."

She did not have the courage and proudly walked past, her eyes fixed on the foliage of the sandbox trees. This memory, together with that of a multitude of minor and major betrayals, probably tortured her up to her death.

After completing the training course, she was assigned to the girls' elementary school at Dubouchage in La Pointe—quite a promotion. It was a huge establishment for its time, the biggest school on the island in number of pupils and classes. She worked there as a schoolmistress for thirty-seven years and people are not yet ready to forget her. Many were the pupils who hated her; many were those who adored her. She left none of them indifferent. At over seventy, Michèle M——, with tears in her eyes, reminded me recently of her status as teacher's pet.

"I was her favorite pupil. After school, I was the one who always carried the homework she had to correct back to her house. At ten o'clock recreation she would send me to fetch her a cup of milk and a buttered slice of bread. Adelia, the maid, would arrange the plate on a little wicker tray that she covered with a doily. I can remember her favorite cup, orangey yellow, decorated with a Japanese lady in a kimono. Her house was filled with lovely things, all sorts of curios I had never seen before."

FOURTEEN

In August, taking advantage of Anne-Marie's dentist appointment, Jeanne made an exception and set foot once again in the house on the rue de Nasssau to inform Victoire she was to be married the following month.

Victoire was in the kitchen cleaning a capon she had the inspiration to stuff with green papayas, cinnamon, and diced bacon.

"*Pouki sa?*" she asked, inspecting surreptitiously her daughter's belly.

"I'm not pregnant," Jeanne reassured her coldly.

That's not the way we do things, her stuffy person and prim posture was saying. So why? What was the hurry? Why was she rushing into marriage? She had just reached twenty. With her physique, her prestige as an elementary school teacher, and, by no means insignificant, her salary, she was an enviable match. She had every freedom to choose and all the time in the world. Auguste Boucolon, Grand Nègre, admittedly could boast of never putting a foot wrong! Brought up by his mama, who was abandoned long before his birth by her seafaring common-law husband, he had proven to be unusually intelligent ever since the local elementary school. He was one of the first to win a scholarship to the Lycée Carnot. Moreover, he was considered good-looking. Supremely well attired. A genuine Beau Brummel with his choice of hats—fedora, boater, and pith helmet—as well as his well-tailored suits. But at the age of forty-two he was older than the mother of his betrothed and already balding, displaying a crown of graying hair. Furthermore, he was a widower, father of two small boys and an illegitimate daughter, conceived while he was a schoolboy, who worked at the registrar's office at city hall and whose mother sold her produce in the market. All that wasn't very romantic!

I was told that despite appearances he was not lacking in lyricism. Apparently, he confided in a friend:

"If I don't have her I'll kill myself."

Going down on one knee, he was reported to have assured her:

"I will be the quilt of your life."

Or else:

"Like Orpheus, I would descend to the ends of the underworld for you if need be."

In his desire to please her, it was said he gave up a ten-year liaison with his mistress, who was convinced she would have a wedding band on her finger after his first wife died. Victoire, who was not at all thrilled by these wedding plans, did not even think of raising an objection. She knew full well she had no say in the matter.

Although the announcement of Jeanne's wedding and her setting up house in La Pointe was to nobody's liking, it drove Boniface to despair. For him it meant one thing: the end of his relationship with Victoire. Jeanne would require it. Furthermore, he knew Victoire was accustomed to obeying and secretly terrified by her daughter. She was not up to defending a love that her daughter considered intolerable and even more despicable than adultery. At night, he tried to win her over. But Victoire as usual didn't say a word.

It was perhaps as a result of this distress, tension, and anguish that he contracted the illness, never clearly diagnosed, which was to carry him off so quickly. Anne-Marie had no qualms spreading the rumor that he was dying of a broken heart, from having been cast aside, something Victoire's detractors were quick to believe.

In a threatening letter, Anne-Marie ordered Jeanne to come and officially introduce her fiancé. Weren't Boniface and herself a sort of adopted parents? They had ensured her education and paid for her schooling. In short, they had made her what she was. They had even provided her with a dowry. Anne-Marie did not know that on his death Boniface had left a legacy for Jeanne. Consequently, to call the modest sum he had placed in her account a dowry was the product of Anne-Marie's exaggerated imagination, which had no bounds. Jeanne grudgingly complied.

Auguste therefore had two magnificent bouquets of roses delivered, one for each of the mothers—the biological and the foster—chocolates for Valérie-Anne, and Havana cigars for the father and son. This did not prevent Boniface Jr. in his jealousy from refusing to attend and going to lunch alone at the Hotel des Postes, where his father had an account. It was at that time he sent Jeanne the letter that I have already mentioned. I don't know whether she answered it. I discovered it over sixty years later in her personal papers.

On the said day, Auguste and Jeanne turned up at the rue de Nassau on the dot, unusual in our climate. Under the avid looks of the servants who were watching the scene from the yard, Auguste removed his boater and with a click of his heels kissed the hand of Anne-Marie.

Mary mother of Jesus! Where on earth did these Negroes learn such things?

Jeanne took off her cotton gloves to show her engagement ring, a good-size diamond, purchased by catalog from the Belles Pierres store in Reims, the French affiliate of a factory in Antwerp. While drinking the Bollinger champagne before the meal, Auguste elaborated his plans and discreetly introduced himself as a good match: a six-room town house and enough to buy a change-of-air house given his solid bank account. It was Anne-Marie who responded, and without her realizing it, unless it was deliberate, her short speech was deeply hurtful. She recalled that without her, without Boniface especially, Jeanne would not have achieved her uncommon status and would probably be speaking a heavy Creole, hiring her services to some bourgeois family, scrubbing their floors and emptying their chamber pots. In exchange for so much kindness she was merely asking for a little respect and gratitude.

Pale with rage, Jeanne had to drink a toast with her.

Victoire had cooked a meal whose menu unfortunately nobody has kept. She arranged it in a lavish dinnerware set as if it were a cooking competition, but left it up to the servants to carry in the dishes. For once, she sat down at the table, to the left of Boniface, as the second Madame Walberg, with Anne-Marie on his right. Auguste laid down once and for all the tone of his relations with Victoire. Given their similar ages, relations should have been fraternal. There was, however, never any intimacy between them. Deep down, she had little sympathy for him, considering him not good enough for her jewel of a daughter, like all mother-in-laws. As for him, we shouldn't be under any illusion. He despised her. Beneath his easygoing manners, he was intolerant, a militant black like all the Grands Nègres, convinced that sexual relations by a woman of color with a white Creole constituted an intolerable scandal. If Fanon had already written *Black Skin White Masks*, Auguste would have certainly appreciated the pages on the complex of lactification. The only agreeable element was when he spoke to Victoire in Creole; in his mouth the language he had also used to speak to his mother took on a different and intimate inflection.

Creole, he seemed to indicate, is our mother tongue, our common link. Let us be proud of it.

Those gathered for this meal didn't have much in common. Fortunately, except for Anne-Marie, who was never at a loss for words, Auguste was capable of talking for two, three, or even four. This feature of his character became increasingly unbearable for Jeanne as she herself became gradually more taciturn and haughty. He spouted anecdote upon anecdote. He told the story, for instance, of how as a student at the Lycée Carnot in 1889 he had been sent to Paris with other Guadeloupeans and Martinicans to visit the Universal Exhibition. He described the amazement of the Parisians when they entered a café or restaurant. How certain customers in a panic rushed for the door. Everyone noisily expressed their astonishment that they knew how to handle a knife and fork. Children cried when approached. Others were bolder and came and rubbed their cheeks to see if the color rubbed off. There were happier moments in the evenings when they went and danced the beguine *wabap* in the Paris dives. His look of nostalgia gave the impression there were other moments of pleasure that he did not mention out of respect for Jeanne. Anne-Marie, who still harbored the regret in her heart of not having completed the years at the conservatoire in Boulogne, inquired about his thoughts on the City of Light. He made a face.

"You know what Jean-Hégésippe Légitimus said about it?"

Anne-Marie and Boniface confessed their ignorance.

"But you know who Jean-Hégésippe Légitimus was, don't you?" he asked with a sudden insolence, staring at them with his sparkling eyes.

How could Anne-Marie and Boniface not know that his Terrible Troisième party had sounded the death knell of the white and mulatto supremacy in Guadeloupe? They stammered a timid yes.

"He said," Auguste declared, "that Paris was too cold and the streets were too busy."

Thereupon he burst out laughing amid the terrified silence at the mention of the name of Légitimus. This was the only false note, albeit minor, we admit, during the entire meal.

The servants then served coffee and cognac in the back garden. Boniface, who had always had a liking for botany, had planted some *Tristellateia australasiae*, whose glowing yellow flowers looked like a multitude of tiny suns.

Fifteen

Auguste and Jeanne were married on September 12, 1910, two weeks before the new school term started. They postponed their honeymoon until the following year, when they planned to visit Paris on a grand scale during the long vacation.

Stubborn as always, confident, she believed, in her right as a benefactor, Anne-Marie took Valérie-Anne by the hand and insisted on going to the wedding ceremony at the new town hall, which had just moved into a lovely eighteenth-century building on the Grand-Rue. Once there, however, she almost turned around and went back, amazed at all these Negro men and women dressed in the latest fashion, speaking French French and making the mother and daughter feel that their presence was out of place. Filled with a kind of terror, she wondered where she could have been when this tsunami had battered the shores of the island. Did she still have a place here? The homily of the deputy mayor, he too a jet-black Negro, frightened her even more. Looking her straight in the eye, he spoke of the time that was coming when the color of the skin would be nothing more than a shadow of the past. White or light skin no longer signified ipso facto accession to privilege.

"That time is *over* and definitely *over*," he thundered.

She clutched Valérie-Anne's hand—Valérie-Anne was equally scared—to give herself a semblance of composure. She was so shaken that back home on the rue de Nassau she went to bed with a migraine and did not attend the religious ceremony at the cathedral. Auguste, though a Freemason true to Légitimus, agreed to the church ceremony to please Jeanne, who would not have accepted a civil wedding. For the reception, miscalculating the extent to which Jeanne was determined to turn her back on her former life, Anne-Marie had offered the house on the rue de Nassau, which with its series of salons would have made a perfect setting. Jeanne hadn't even taken the trouble to reply. She chose the Grand Hotel des Antilles, which had just opened its doors. This magnificent establishment appeared to be the sign of things to come. It was situated at the corner of the rue Sadi-Carnot and the rue Schoelcher. Telephone and running water in every room, it publicized. Access to the salons was through a garden where Chinese fan palms, introduced at great cost, and purple flower crape myrtle grew. The salons themselves were decorated with an array of potted palms and ixoras.

For the first time Victoire wore a European-style dress. A drape of prune-colored crepe de Chine that Jeanne had ordered from a catalog at La Samaritaine in Paris. She had to have it altered by a dressmaker, since Victoire was so small and slender. Such finery showed off her beauty: an unusual beauty. An insidious beauty that the eye did not see at first. A beauty spoiled by the lack of confidence in herself, the conviction of her unworthiness, and the awkwardness that comes with it. People who vainly tried to converse with her whispered that she could have borrowed a little assurance from her daughter, who with enough to spare had made herself obnoxious. What they didn't know was that outwardly so different, Victoire and Jeanne were identical. Like mother, like daughter. Both tormented souls scared stiff of their surroundings.

Victoire would have liked to proclaim her love for her daughter in the only way she was capable of—by preparing a meal more extravagant than that of the engagement. A meal where she could display her treasure chest of inventions. The menu was there in her head like the draft of a novel that will testify to the genius of its author. But Jeanne did not want to treat her mother like a servant. She insisted on hiring a caterer by the name of Soudon who dispatched a maître d' and a dozen waiters in white starched uniforms. She sat Victoire in the middle of the room like an Akan queen mother in a magnificent armchair. All that was missing was the parasol over her head.

Victoire felt extremely ill at ease with all these eyes on her. Like an adulterous woman, she waited to be stoned. Among the guests, nobody had committed a sin like hers.

The guests whirled around to the sound and rhythm of the waltzes from Paris performed by an orchestra that serenaded as best it could. At eleven forty-five it stopped playing. The dancers made a circle around Auguste and Jeanne. Auguste then made a speech. First of all he paid homage to his mother, who had not lived to see this day. Then he turned to his mother-in-law, who had fashioned the jewel of which he, the most fortunate of men, was taking possession. He made the mistake of using the same words to celebrate both women: valiant, feisty, belligerent, and pillars of society. The fabrication was obvious. Then the violinists played the habanera from *Carmen:*

> *L'amour est un oiseau rebelle,*
> *Que nul ne peut apprivoiser,*
> *Et c'est bien en vain qu'on l'appelle*
> *S'il lui convient de refuser.*

There was a storm of applause. A genuine ovation. Yet it was nothing but pure hypocrisy. Most of the guests knew the cards had been dealt wrongly, that Victoire in no way deserved such praise. However, more than Auguste's lying hyperboles, it was the musical interlude that gave great displeasure. Was Jeanne Boucolon—it was surely her idea—in her right mind? To have Georges Bizet's opera played for her mother, her illiterate and uneducated mother! Why not Johann Sebastian Bach? Who was she trying to delude? Everyone knew Jeanne. She always thought she was the cat's whiskers. But this time, she had crossed the line.

Shortly after midnight, a car drove the couple to the rue de Condé. The rue de Condé is situated on the other side of the Place de la Victoire, and until the emergence of a black bourgeoisie, it defined the limits of the town's habitable perimeter. In this emerging neighborhood Auguste owned a modest one-story house with a balcony and attic—nothing like the one he had built on the rue Alexandre Isaac shortly before I was born. He had lived there for ten years with his first wife, now deceased. The new couple settled in amid the debris of a first love.

At last, Auguste could savor Jeanne's body, which he had lusted after so desperately. There was no *griotte* to hang out the wrappers stained with blood. But she was a virgin, that's for sure. I don't know what my mother thought of her wedding night or any of the following nights. What I do know is that I never heard her broach the subject of sex—which is unusual, even exceptional in our islands—without some measure of disgust.

One week later, it was Boniface's turn at the wheel of his Cleveland to take Victoire to the rue de Condé. He loaded onto his shoulder like a porter the trunk containing her old clothes. In this quiet neighborhood the intrusion of the Cleveland produced the same effect as in Le Moule: people came out on their balconies or on their doorsteps to contemplate this high-powered car. They had much to be amazed about. What was this white Creole doing at the Boucolons? Who was this mulatto woman with him? Jeanne's mother? She looked like a woman from Les Saintes. Did she come from Terre-de-Haut? From that moment on, the gossip began to rage.

The unfortunate Boniface had put time to his advantage. Night after night, he attempted to prove to Victoire the sanctity of their relations. Since she listened to him without saying a word, he did not know whether he had convinced her. In despair he was prepared to talk to Jeanne himself. He was not asking for much. Just so they would let him see his Victoire from time to time. But confronted with Jeanne's impenetrable and contemptuous expression, he realized she would not listen to reason. So he kept silent and stumbled out of the house.

Jeanne had prepared for her mother the best room in the house: on the second floor, opening onto a balcony, since she did not want to relegate her to the attic under the roof like a servant. In order to climb into the four-poster bed *à boules,* you had to use a small pair of steps. The highlight of the furnishing was without doubt an oval cheval glass, surmounted by a decorative motif on an ornate frame, which gave a full-length reflection. The emotion and gratitude that such munificence could have caused Victoire was largely tempered by the conversation that followed. Jeanne calmly reiterated what she had already said in Le Moule. In the world she was entering, her association with a white Creole was unacceptable. *Intolerable.* No more commerce of the flesh or anything else. No mixing with company that might invite malicious gossip. Just as Caesar's wife should be above suspicion, so the mother and mother-in-law of a Grand Nègre should be unassailable. The white Creoles were our enemies. They had subjugated and whipped their slaves for generations. They had only one desire at heart: humiliate the blacks by every means possible and reduce them to the level of animals.

Even if it had been said in Japanese, the effect of this short speech would have been the same. Victoire was incapable of understanding it. She did not know the meaning of the words "class" or "exploiters." In her eyes, the Walbergs were not enemies: neither Anne-Marie nor Boniface. She didn't dare say they were her friends. To use an out-of-date term that would have made Jeanne's blood boil, they had always behaved like good masters.

I admit I have difficulty accepting the fact that Victoire relinquished Boniface so easily—her companion for twenty years who had given her pleasure, who had forgiven her infidelity, who had looked after her child, and who in a manner of speaking considered

Victoire his only reason for living. I refuse, however, to accept the theory generally acknowledged by the inhabitants of La Pointe that since Victoire could get nothing more out of Boniface, she shamelessly turned her back on him. I believe that once again the fear instilled by her daughter got the upper hand. She could not envisage for one moment standing up to her at the risk of displeasing her. There is no doubt whatsoever the thought of Boniface tormented her, denying her sleep. I can see her at night with her eyes wide open in the dark, tossing and turning in her bed, thinking of her partner. I can imagine her in the midst of her daily routine suddenly gripped by his memory and obliged to stop for fear of bursting into tears.

Boniface never came back to the rue de Condé and Jeanne could claim that his relations with her mother were now over and done with. At Christmas and New Year's he faithfully sent Victoire expensive presents, one of which was one of the first radio sets of the time.

I find it surprising that Jeanne never intervened likewise in the relations between her mother and Anne-Marie. She probably dreaded Anne-Marie, knowing her to be a loudmouth, capable of making terrible scenes. The fact remains, however, that Victoire and Anne-Marie continued to meet every day on the Place de la Victoire. To my knowledge, Boniface respected Jeanne's instructions and never came to join them.

LIFE, THEREFORE, WAS organized without Boniface.

On the rue de Condé everything revolved around Jeanne's teaching. She would get up at four in the morning, leaving Auguste lounging in bed. At that time, I don't know why, she had given up daily mass, something she was to take up again only after Victoire died. She gave the final touches to her lessons and finished correcting the homework. Then she did an hour's gymnastics in order to lose weight. Abdominals especially. Or else, dressed in one of her husband's old pair of shorts, she would run as far as the harbor. Showing off her legs at her age was a bold step and the churchgoers coming home from first mass looked at her reproachfully. Her reputation for being odd started to be without precedent. Everything she did caused a sensation. What was this idea of running to lose weight? A woman should be proud to show off her curves, a sign that she is being spoiled at home.

Back at the rue de Condé, she would shower—Auguste's running water was his pride and joy—dress, and rig herself out with jewels. She would down a huge bowl of coffee, without sugar, prepared by Victoire, who had been up since dawn. We should say in passing that this coffee without sugar was another oddity on an island with such a sweet tooth. Then she left for school. It was seven o'clock, the sun had begun to open wide its eyes, and Auguste was scarcely out of bed. She was keen to arrive at school ahead of time so that she could write on the blackboard in her fine, well-rounded writing the math problems or questions of grammar.

Since there was no lacking in household staff, two servants and a *mabo* for Auguste's two boys, Victoire found herself in the same situation as in Le Moule: she had nothing to do all day. This time, she took the bull by the horns and tried hard to invent things to do for herself. She supervised the housework, tracing the dust over the furniture with her finger. When the servants came back from market, she inspected their baskets, weighing again the pork for casserole on an old pair of Roberval scales and checking every cent of the expenses. In the afternoon, she would mend clothes, sew buttons on shirts, and darn socks, things that Jeanne, brought up by the Walbergs as a young lady, was incapable of doing. Then she made sure the washing was well starched and ironed, ruthless about creases in Auguste's shirt cuffs and collars. Very soon the servants began to loathe Victoire, who was always on their backs. She was the cause of a stream of girls being taken on a trial basis, hired, then dismissed, all uttering the same complaints as they turned in their aprons: the mistress thought she was God's gift to mankind, but the mother was worse: a real shrew.

As for meals, Auguste was not much different from Jeanne. He was capable of lunching off a slice of yam soaked in a spoonful of olive oil and rubbed with a piece of cod or smoked herring, a souvenir of his childhood as a *maléré*. Victoire however gave him the taste for fine cooking. Henceforth, he sat down at the table for lunch with a napkin around his neck like a child and was served grilled lobster tails or smoked chicken in lemongrass under the disdainful eye of Jeanne, who pecked away at her purslane salad.

"My favorite dishes," he recalled, on the rare occasions when he talked about his mother-in-law, something he was always reticent to do, I don't know why, "were not the complicated ones of her invention where she mixed all sorts of spices, sweet and sour, meat and seafood. It was the way she made a simple fish broth with tench and grunt, rice, cow peas, and a sliver of salt pork. For me that was a feast."

Auguste was the only one in the household to be spared criticism by the servants and the neighbors' gossip. They pitied him, rather, having to live with such a mother-in-law and married to a shrew he was incapable of taming. In actual fact, contrary to what people thought, he was somewhat hard-hearted and indifferent to anything that didn't concern Jeanne or himself. He never shared his wife's idealism on the values of secular education nor the generous aspirations of the Grands Nègres who claimed to lead the entire Race onward. His only concern was to make money. He spent his time satisfying the obscure dreams of a child born in a hovel on the Morne à Cayes and finished up brandishing his cutlass, dressed in khakis, and playing the gentleman farmer and banana planter on his property in Sarcelles.

The round of visits to the Grands Nègres in La Pointe, however, was just as imperative as in Le Moule and also took place on Sunday afternoons, since high mass at the cathedral of Saint-Pierre and Saint-Paul took up the mornings, dress preparations and gossiping in front of the church included. Edgar Littée, a bourgeois mulatto, had the idea of capturing on film daily scenes in the life of this society of mimicry in La Pointe: a riot of drapes and wide-brimmed hats, little boys dressed in sailor suits and the girls in frilly dresses. Here and there a black face, if we don't include the *mabos*, the nursemaids. In La Pointe the club of Grands Nègres was more closely organized. Its members all lived in close proximity to one another, in a neighborhood situated symbolically far from the white Creoles, but also far from the stench of the outlying district where the *maléré* lodged.

When I returned to Pointe-à-Pitre after an absence of twenty years, I realized I had practically never crossed the Vatable Canal. All I knew of the town was the narrow quadrilateral where I had been brought up. I had to go back and discover its shacks, its yards, and its storm channels swarming with guppies.

In actual fact, the members of the club of Grands Nègres were never very many in number. As the years went by, it became increasingly difficult to join. It was no longer just a question of education or being one of the first physicians or first teachers. Apart from the basic rules of occupying a certain position in society, living in an upstairs-downstairs house, speaking only French, and having been at least once to France and stayed in Paris, more subtler edicts were proclaimed. Monsieur Cabriou, for instance, magistrate, who roared with laughter in the most vulgar way, displaying the pink velvet of his uvula, and whose wife sat on enormous buttocks, was excluded forever. More than in Le Moule, Victoire loathed these visits. Alas, she was forced to accompany Auguste and Jeanne on every one of them, walking three steps behind them. She sat without a smile or a word, never answering questions, turning her glass of grenadine round and round in her hands. Soon an even more terrible ordeal loomed.

Together with a group of Grands Nègres, Auguste planned to establish a bank, the Caisse Coopérative des Prêts, which was the exact name for this institution that in fact was quite modest. The members of the future board of directors decided on a weekly dinner with their wives. Wasn't sitting round a table for a meal the most convivial way of getting to know one another? Auguste and Jeanne, who had an outstanding cook at home, offered to be the hosts for such gatherings. I believe the idea was Auguste's; he was afraid that his mother-in-law was finding life on the rue de Condé somewhat empty. Like at Anne-Marie's, Victoire found herself in the position of a writer forced to honor a commission from her publisher. Very quickly, her work weighs heavy on her, becomes unbearable and a chore. For cooking, like writing, can only blossom in an atmosphere of total freedom and cannot stand constraints. The devil with rules, treatises, manifestos, and poetic arts. Paradoxically, Jeanne was constantly on her back, overwhelming her with suggestions.

"How about cooking your splendid stew of crayfish in lemon and green mangoes? Or your guinea fowl with currants and honey?"

"No! Whatever they pretend, those people have no palate. Just do a chicken fricassee served with a gratin of green golden apples."

"No! Rather pork with saffron and coconut milk served with Creole rice."

Victoire complied, without sulking and without betraying any grudge. It would have been all right if she could have stayed in the kitchen with the servants facing the dishes she had contrived to cook. But once again Jeanne forced her to get dressed, sit in the drawing room with the guests, sit down at the table with them, and listen to an incomprehensible conversation in which she was incapable of taking part. However much the guests heaped compliments on her, she got the feeling she was not in her place. The devotion that Jeanne showed her at those meals appeared to her ostentatious and theatrical. She was convinced it was nothing but a smokescreen designed to conceal to what degree she was ashamed of her. So she hunkered down at the end of the table, silent and sickened, offering the sight of her profound distress to one and all.

"Poor Madame Quidal! You do feel sorry for her!" commented the diners back home with a full stomach, having eaten their fill.

"What can you expect with a daughter like that. She's a real pain!"

We would be wrong in thinking that Jeanne, like Anne-Marie at the time, got any pleasure out of these weekly gatherings. For her too, but for different reasons, they were torture. It was not just the smell from the mounds of food that turned her stomach together with the sight of the so-called distinguished guests stuffing themselves greedily, Auguste worst of all. What an appetite he had! It was because she was the youngest of the group. They treated her like a child who meddles with grown-up affairs instead of minding her own business. She suggested for instance that the future employees of the Caisse Coopérative des Prêts wear badges with their names on them. A ridiculous idea! Some of them had known the first Madame Boucolon, Antoinette Sambalas, and hinted that she was far better than the second. Less beautiful. Less elegant. Less educated, that's for sure—she was merely a salesgirl in the haberdashery department of the store Au Dernier Chic—but that didn't mean she wasn't less adorable, less agreeable, and she knew where a woman's place was.

As you can see, life on the rue de Condé was not exactly pleasant. Auguste, who in his time had been quite a lad, had turned over a new leaf. After school was over, he was always home reading his newspaper or watching the crowd in the street from the balcony. In private he did not bother Jeanne with his stories, since she took no interest in them. The one exception to his staid ways was his Montecristo cigars he ordered from Cuba, on which he had his initials, AB, printed on the ring. As for Jeanne, she never stopped working. She would buy the teacher's answer books and immerse herself into the key to exercises. As for Victoire, she dreamed. About what?

As you can see, there was no music or reading. My father ordered books, a little like he ordered champagne, from the House of Nelson, who shipped the entire works of an author. All of La Fontaine. All of Molière. All of Lamartine. These were hardbacks with a white cover. Once he had arranged them on the library shelves he never touched them again. I can recall having read at the age of ten all the plays of Victor Hugo. *Le roi s'amuse* made a deep impression on me.

AT THIS TIME, apart from Anne-Marie, Victoire began to keep company with a person who could have been of great comfort to her. Alas, the relationship was short-lived.

Her name was Jeanne Repentir, and she was somewhat of an eccentric. She had arrived from New Orleans five years earlier and had opened a dressmaker's shop under the name of the Golden Thimble, a modest sign hung on the door of a modest lodging. Jeanne Repentir quickly became the darling of the black and mulatto coquettes of La Pointe, since with the help of a little dark girl from the outlying districts, two mannequins, and a few patterns from the *Modes et Travaux* collection, she managed to give an inimitable touch to her creations.

Victoire had accompanied her daughter one day for a fitting and the two women had got along well with each other.

They had a good many things in common.

Both from Marie-Galante, they had left their native island very young and had never returned. They had no idea what white man had fathered them, though Jeanne Repentir liked to claim, with no grounds whatsoever, that he was a Basque country gentleman with a double-barreled name as long as your arm. But what would a Basque country gentleman with a double-barreled name as long as your arm be doing in Marie-Galante at the end of the nineteenth century? In any case, I could find no trace of him in the archives. They were so light-skinned that even the eye of a Guadeloupean, expert in detecting the slightest degree of color, could be mistaken. Jeanne Repentir had bluish purple eyes; Victoire's, as we know, were pale gray.

In an almost identical manner, they had both got pregnant by a black male. As for Gratien Philogène, Jeanne Repentir's short-lived partner, he had recognized his daughter. However, he had taken so little care of her that he had let her die of tuberculosis at the age of thirteen, whereas he could have had her treated in a sanatorium in France. After that Jeanne Repentir had fallen madly in love with Gervais de Puyrode, a white Creole from Martinique, owner at the time of the Courcelles sugar factory in Sainte-Anne. Barely escaping the fire that burned down his property, Gervais, together with Jeanne and Vitalis, his newborn son, took refuge on the White Mango estate not far from New Orleans. Passion doesn't last, it's a well-known fact. Cradling Vitalis in her arms, Jeanne Repentir was soon back in Guadeloupe, where, taking advantage of her travel experiences, she set up her own business. As for Vitalis, he was so handsome, blond and curly-haired, that the priests would choose him every year to crown the Virgin Mary during the August 15 celebrations at the cathedral of Saint-Pierre and Saint-Paul. Apart from that, he was a little brat who broke his mother's heart by playing hooky and spending his time fighting the little ragamuffins in the Vatable Canal district. Jeanne Repentir lived in expectation of a letter from Gervais, who would bring her back to White Mango, where she and her son would take up their rightful place. She had seen this moment in her dreams and her dreams never lied.

Other things separated them. One of them was fundamental.

Since her mother's family had not lacked presence of mind, Jeanne Repentir had been educated and knew how to read and write. Her invoices, written in blue ink on squared mauve stationery (my mother kept several of them), were proof of it. She spoke the most refined French, at times a little affected. The two women so alike yet so different would often meet in the afternoons in Jeanne Repentir's home, composed of four rooms, since the living room was divided in two by a cretonne drape behind which the fittings took place. Victoire sat head lowered over the hems that Jeanne Repentir gave her to overcast, listening intently to her friend's phantasmagorical tales.

"New Orleans," she recounted, turning nonchalantly the handle of her Singer sewing machine, "believe me, I never liked that city. It's built on the stench of the swamps. As soon as dusk falls, there's a terrible smell and humidity oozes out of everywhere. You can't even bury the dead for fear the bodies will emerge from the mud and come back to haunt the living.

"I left because of the yellow fever epidemic that broke out that year. I had never seen anything like it. They would cover the heaps of corpses with quicklime and burn them on the sidewalks, in the storm channels and in the yards. What with the stench of the swamps, you can imagine what it was like. Of course there are some things I miss. In the French market, they used to sell bananas as red as pomegranates, grapes as sticky as dates, china, porcelain, and picaninnies tattooed like monkeys."

Having nothing as juicy to recount, Victoire brought desserts that she knew Jeanne Repentir was particularly fond of.

"I've got a sweet tooth!" she laughed, showing off her English.

A mamee apple pound cake. A soufflé of ripe papaya. A custard flan with cashew fruit from La Désirade.

"You're a poet, a poet," Jeanne Repentir would say, biting greedily into these small wonders. "You don't know it, but you're so much better than your daughter."

She too didn't like Jeanne very much, although she was one of her best customers. Not that she took offense because Jeanne was jealous of her friendship with Victoire. That's how children are. But she knew that despite her white skin and her sojourn in the United States, Jeanne looked down upon her. A dressmaker! A subaltern!

When she didn't have any urgent orders, she would accompany Victoire to the Place de la Victoire, where they met up with Anne-Marie. In the shade of the music kiosk, there was a court-bouillon of gossip, as the saying goes, that Victoire had no other choice but to swallow.

"If she keeps puffing herself up like a peacock, Jeanne will burst!" Jeanne Repentir guffawed.

"She's like the frog who aspires to become bigger than the ox!" chimed in Anne-Marie, remembering her La Fontaine fables.

Anne-Marie never suggested Victoire return to live on the rue de Nassau, for she knew Victoire would never accept it, but she made no mystery of what she thought of the life Victoire was leading at her daughter's.

"They'll kill you. All that counts for them," she declared in contempt, "is appearances. They've got no real feelings."

Suddenly the unexpected occurred and the incredible dream came true. At death's door following a fall from his horse, Gervais de Puyrode sent for Jeanne Repentir and Vitalis with the intention of putting himself in God's good graces before the final reckoning by marrying the mother and legitimizing the son. Within a week the deliveries were completed, and the Golden Thimble emptied of all its contents. Even the sewing machine found a buyer. Late one afternoon Anne-Marie and Victoire sadly accompanied Jeanne and Vitalis, who embarked for New York on board the SS *Valparaiso*. From there they would take the train south to New Orleans. Under the almond trees on the Foulon wharf, Anne-Marie and Jeanne Repentir cried their hearts out while Victoire stood to one side, dry-eyed, yet just as deeply distressed. Was it the end of their friendship? Would they ever see each other again? On this point Jeanne Repentir was categorical. She could not imagine her life without visiting Guadeloupe. *Pawol sé van*, goes the proverb! Yes, words are a lot of wind and hot air. Weeks, months went by. Mother and son were never heard of again. Not even a hurriedly scribbled letter or cheap card. Jeanne Repentir and Vitalis seemed to have disappeared into a ghostly limbo.

A few years ago I was invited by Tulane University and made the mandatory rounds of the plantation houses in Louisiana. However hard I pressed my guides with questions, nobody had ever heard of White Mango or of a family from Guadeloupe who was said to have settled there at the beginning of the twentieth century. Wasn't it rather a family of Haitians? There were plenty of those, especially in the region of Lafayette. I ended my stay no wiser.

Was the information I got from my mother pure fantasy?

Nobody knows what Victoire felt when the person who helped color the gray of her days left. She became neither more morose nor more withdrawn. Her daily routine set in once again.

Fortunately, at the end of December, her daughter gave her the most wonderful of gifts. She announced that she would not be able to travel to France during the long vacation. God had decided otherwise. He had blessed their union.

She was expecting a baby in July.

SIXTEEN

1911 began therefore as a year of grace.

The neighbors, watching Victoire come and go, noticed that she seemed less stressed, to use a current expression. With less reprimands, the servants played along. Tensions and resentment seemed forgotten.

In fact, under her impassive air, Victoire was overjoyed.

"Marvel of marvels! My daughter is pregnant! The woman I carried inside me is now carrying her own child. A little stranger has taken refuge inside her. It's breathing and feeding thanks to her. In nine months we shall know its face. Marvel of marvels!"

This belly that was miraculously swelling was a bond of sweetness that tied her to her daughter.

Only spoiled women experience painful pregnancies. The others don't have the time. From the very first months, Jeanne was tortured by nausea, vomiting, and dizzy spells. Once she even fainted in a store where she was ordering the lawn and lace of her layette. Victoire did not spare her efforts. Twenty times a day she ran to the Dubouchage school to take her all kinds of herb teas: greasy bush, couch grass, semicontract, worm grass, old maid, and rock balsam that ensure the equilibrium of the body. The most extraordinary thing was that Jeanne got her appetite back, possessed once again of those cravings she hadn't had since the age of reason. Victoire responded with devotion, feeling at last avenged for so many years of indifference. She would lovingly prepare chicken breasts, veal cutlets, and fish fillets. She cooked up purees and breadfruit stews. She especially strived hard to make desserts, puddings, creams, and flans, since pregnant women need excess sugar to nourish the brain.

Despite her health, Jeanne refused any kind of sick leave and, pushing her belly in front of her, walked with difficulty to the Dubouchage school. She had too high an opinion of the importance of her job to pamper herself. For her it was more than a mission. It was a calling. She had suffered so much humiliation in the religious establishments where she had been educated that she was convinced of the need for a secular, republican education.

Seeing her walk past, elderly gossips who claimed to be clairvoyant announced she would have a daughter: her belly had the shape of a full moon. That would have pleased Auguste. But she would angrily hear nothing of the sort. Her child would be a boy. His name would be Auguste, like his father, and would lay the first stone of the "Boucolon dynasty." One might argue that the Boucolon dynasty was already well established: Auguste's first two sons already bore the name. But she attached no importance to them whatsoever— they complained bitterly about it later on—and considered them at best as two bastards. Despite the bush teas and baths, Jeanne was no better. Her legs were heavy and stiff with cramps at night. Nightmares would wake her up. One of them in particular: she was making her way through the roots and trees of a mangrove swamp. She did not know who was steering the boat and she was scared. The boatman's face was hidden under a hood like a member of the Ku Klux Klan. Suddenly the boat overturned and she was floundering in the mud.

So as not to disturb Auguste, she transferred her night things to a little room in the attic that Victoire came to share with her.

These were moments of intimacy that perhaps mother and daughter had previously never known and were never to know again. Jeanne had seldom seen her mother undressed, without her ungainly head-tie, with her long, straight schoolgirl's hair reaching down to her shoulders. Like a little kid, she got great fun passing a comb back and forth through Victoire's hair. She became permeated with her subtle sensuality, vaguely envying her, for she had always been convinced she herself had no sex appeal. She all too often had been a wallflower at the afternoon dances in Basse-Terre, where they sometimes went, unbeknown to the nuns. No bashful lover, frantic with desire, had waited for her behind the boarding school wall. I am convinced that the only man she had made love to was my father. If she felt any passion, she controlled it very closely and let nothing show.

Victoire for her part only knew her daughter in her Sunday best, decked out, made up, and caparisoned. She now saw her without makeup, her hair disheveled, in a crumpled nightdress, and it was as if she had become a little girl again. She would bathe her, tenderly passing the sponge over the heavy fruit of her belly and massaging her with a glove soaked in a mixture of camphorated alcohol and turpentine. At the same time she would speak to her silently:

"I know you're not happy, in spite of your upstairs-downstairs house, your diamond engagement ring, your torsade wedding band, and your jewel box, which keeps getting heavier thanks to Auguste. It's my fault, my very own fault. As soon as you drank my milk, everything changed for the worse. Instead of breathing strength into you, it contaminated you with my malaise and my fears. And now I'm poisoning your life. Besides, haven't I always poisoned it, thinking I was doing the right thing? You deserve another mother."

To be sure, Dernier would win hands down in the game of who's to blame. His absence had made Jeanne vulnerable, creating in her the urge for security and respectability, which was increasingly to govern her decisions and take away any spontaneity. Yet Victoire could never free herself from a violent feeling of guilt. Jeanne was what she was because Victoire was what she was.

Bringing a child into this world at the time was exclusively the business of women. A handful of midwives, whose services were much sought after, delivered women from the bourgeoisie at home. But as we have seen, Jeanne was not afraid to be daring. She therefore called on a man, Dr. Mélas. This Grand Nègre, first of all a general practitioner, had studied obstetrics at the University of Port-au-Prince in Haiti. Given the ostracism that reigned in France at the time, Haiti fully enjoyed its role as cultural capital. The Guadeloupeans and Martinicans flocked there to obtain the diplomas they were barred from elsewhere. At the hospital in Jérémie his patients called him tenderly Papa Doc. His very simple techniques were nevertheless revolutionary. As soon as he took charge of Jeanne, she was transformed. He taught her to breathe. He initiated her into gymnastics and prescribed brisk walks; before its time, he was a firm believer in jogging.

With Victoire by her side she jogged as far as the Jardin d'Essai that had just been created in Les Abymes, a conglomeration that today is virtually an extension of Point-à-Pitre, but at that time was rustic and wooded. They would bend down together to smell the perfume from the beds of strange flowers: the milkweed asclepiad from Curacao, the aloe, and the Erythrina, commonly known as cockspur, because of its brilliant cherry-red flowers. However, it was a little too long and tiring for Jeanne, who preferred to walk up the rue Victor Hughes and slowly climb the hillock where the general hospital and the Massabielle church stand today. The top of the hill was overrun by a stunted wood and a savanna of thornbushes. The place was fairly disreputable, where homeless lovers met. You could see them wildly embracing each other in the bushes. From up there you had a wonderful view over to the coast of Basse-Terre and the phosphorescent plateau of the sea, the infinite ambiguous ocean encircling two islands that had marked Victoire's life: Marie-Galante, land of her birth, and Martinique, land of her lost love. Life is nothing but a series of decisions that always prove to be unsatisfactory. Although she never called into question her decision to leave Martinique, ashamed of having nurtured the idea of abandoning her daughter, she sometimes regretted Marie-Galante and the life she thought fit to turn her back on. She began idealizing it like in a Creole novel. When all is said and done, what had she gained by following Anne-Marie's suggestions and settling down with a family of white Creoles in La Pointe? Neither she nor Jeanne had gone hungry. And that's about it. But the poor child bore scars that no surgery could repair.

When the first gas lamps began to dot La Pointe with light, mother and daughter would retrace their steps back to the rue de Condé arm in arm. Thanks to the treatment prescribed by Dr. Mélas, Jeanne had no trouble giving birth. In a few hours, the child came into this world on July 7, 1911. A boy. Fairly ugly. One wondered where he got his drooping lower lip and flat nose from. Joking as usual, his father maintained that a man has no need for beauty. Given the size of his appendage, he could swear that he would know how to please the ladies. Jeanne was not amused. She did not like dirty stories and was visibly vexed at having given birth to this ungainly infant.

As for Victoire, she was in seventh heaven. She saw none of the imperfections that were so obvious to the outsider. That boy was her daughter's, therefore the most perfect and adorable son in the world. At night she would slip into his room to spy on his breathing. During the day, she would take him in her arms as soon as Jeanne had her back turned, for Jeanne, full of modern ideas, ardent reader of the Catholic journal *J'élève mon enfant*, was of the opinion that babies should be given a strict routine, a bottle of milk every three hours, alternating with a bottle of apple juice or filtered water, and never be taken out of their cradle for the slightest reason. In short, Victoire was so happy that one day she persuaded the *mabo* nursemaid on the quiet to take the baby to Anne-Marie on the Place de la Victoire. Unfortunately, Anne-Marie did not like babies. Her nostrils were tickled by their disagreeable smell.

"They smell of shit and Jean-Marie Farina cologne," she claimed. "A horrible mixture."

Deep down, she found the baby a little too black and puny in his sumptuous smocked blouse, but out of fear of hurting her, she said nothing to Victoire.

Ever since the departure of Jeanne Repentir, Victoire and Anne-Marie had been left to themselves. They listened to the municipal concerts together. Since Anne-Marie, who never stopped eating grilled peanuts, was suffering from the first signs of obesity, she believed that walking round the square several times would be a way of fighting it. Soon out of breath, she would sit down on a bench facing the harbor, admiring the serenity of the pink and gray sky. They would listen to the cathedral bells and part around seven thirty.

THE BIRTH OF their first son and the christening as sumptuous as a wedding that followed—there were as many as three hundred guests—consolidated the entrance of Jeanne and Auguste into the club of Grands Nègres. I don't know why, they became one of the most highly regarded couples in La Pointe. I say I don't know why because I must confess I have difficulty understanding the reasons for this preeminence. They did not excel in any particular field or show any specific talent. The Grands Nègres established a cultural association, Alizés, which published a somewhat pretentious rag called *Trait d'Union*. I cannot see my father's signature anywhere. My mother has signed two rather uninteresting articles written with very little imagination. One defends the need for a democratic and secular education—her pet subject. The other is an obituary of one of her colleagues who died giving birth at the age of twenty-five. Apart from that, they never expressed a political opinion and never took part in any major cause. Perhaps it was simply because of appearances. They formed a handsome couple. Both tall, slender, and satisfied with themselves.

For the christening lunch Jeanne called on a Lebanese caterer, a certain Maalouf, who initiated the bourgeoisie, tired of Creole cooking, into the delights of the Middle East: tabbouleh, hummus, and boned duck stuffed with olives. Just as for her wedding, she refused to treat her mother like a servant and burden her with a responsibility that probably would have been too heavy for her. Once again, however, her intentions were misunderstood. Victoire felt excluded, although she carried her grandson to the baptismal font. The newborn was wrapped in a blouse of batiste and Valenciennes lace, several meters long. A fluted frill bonnet hugged his little lackluster face. The godparents were of course two carefully selected Grands Nègres. What mattered were appearances. On every birthday they ritually gave their godchild a small wad of crackling brand-new banknotes. Nothing more. No sign of affection. No special consideration.

Auguste Jr. had the bad idea to be born nine months, almost to the day, before Jean, Jeanne's second son, who was as splendid as a star, his mother would proudly repeat. Auguste Jr. was first of all his father's favorite, but dropped out of favor when he showed no inclination for physical activities and too much liking for unreadable books: Auguste, who had done brilliantly in sports at school, dreamed of a volleyball or football champion for a son. The family legend goes that at age twelve Auguste Jr. would sit on the balcony reading Tacitus and Pliny the Elder in the original. His bedside book was Descartes' *Discours de la Méthode*, from which he could recite entire pages. He had an exceptionally successful university career. The first Guadeloupean to pass the high-level *agrégation* exam. The first black teacher in a prestigious Parisian lycée. Unfortunately, he was never a rebel like his contemporary Aimé Césaire, who, moreover, knew him. Although he courted the muse, his literary talents were lacking and he spent his days, childless and anonymous, among his pink and blonde wife's Pomeranian dogs in the suburb of Asnières.

Thank goodness for Auguste! He was the only one of us who remembered or thought he remembered Victoire. For all of us, this strange-colored grandmother was half imaginary. A spirit. A ghost.

Floating in the mist of time long, long ago. At most an enigmatic photo placed on top of a piano. He remembered the contours of a face as white and gentle as the moon that leaned over his cradle. He claimed that in accordance with the horrible custom of the time, they made him kiss her on her deathbed. He was barely four, but he still shivered as he recalled his terror when he saw the person he adored transformed into a cadaverous object. She never left his side. When he reached the age of piano lessons with M. Démon, the mulatto, who taught all of us our scales, her hand guided his tortured fingers over the ivory and ebony keys. Later on, like Victoire, he adored opera.

Especially the *Carmen* he saw staged all over the world: in Paris, London, Madrid, Tokyo, and Sydney. Victim of the family virus, he traveled a lot. Every time the opera singer started singing the melody he was particularly fond of, a mysterious voice would accompany the words in his ear:

> *L'amour est enfant de Bohême*
> *Il n'a jamais, jamais connu de loi*

SEVENTEEN

The rainy season following Auguste's birth was so wet that people remembered it for years to come. The tropical waves, not yet known by this poetical name but simply as "stormy weather" or "blows," came one after another. The children of the needy *maléré* drowned while floating their roughly made rafts in the canal that had overflowed. One evening Anne-Marie urgently sent for Victoire.

Boniface was very sick.

For months he had suffered from agues, anginas, and hemorrhagic dengue fevers. At present a banal urinary infection was causing blood poisoning and the doctor believed he would not survive the night.

Braving the rain, Victoire ran frantically to the rue de Nassau, where she hadn't set foot for over a year. On arrival she scrambled up the stairs.

Boniface was lying in the Regency room where they had spent so many nights together. When she came in, he regained consciousness and burst into tears. He was unrecognizable, all skin and bone. Perhaps she had never realized until then the place she occupied in his life nor the one he occupied in her heart. Boniface was a man of few manners, had difficulty expressing himself, was incapable of formulating the emotions she inspired in him, and was somewhat shy. All of a sudden she realized that her absence was killing him and that perhaps she too would die from it. However hard she deployed her panoply of bush teas, herb teas, decoctions, poultices, emetics, and purgatives, nothing helped and his condition worsened. After two heart attacks, he passed away.

If Boniface had been a beggar, nobody would have given him a thought. He had not accomplished anything memorable, nothing that would go down in history. By making money out of selling codfish, he had built up a considerable fortune: one of the biggest on the island.

As a consequence, a flotilla of white Creoles with the appropriate expression invaded his house for the wake. I say white Creoles because the island society was reluctant to integrate. Only two or three mulattos were to be seen amid the gathering. As for the blacks, the only ones present were the store employees from the Lardenoy wharf. Overdressed and ill at ease, they hastily recited a dozen rosaries in front of the corpse and hurriedly exited to soak their soles in the puddles. Everyone presented their condolences to Anne-Marie, half hidden under her mourning veils, surrounded by her two children, who, like their mother, had no idea what attitude to adopt. Boniface Jr. had theoretically loved his father but had never paid him much attention. Valérie-Anne was mainly frightened. Didn't the dead come and tickle your feet? Anne-Marie, who had made no mystery of her lack of sentiment for her husband, felt merely that strange fear we all feel in the vicinity of death.

They ignored Victoire, the only person to be truly unhappy, haggard and red-eyed, who together with the servants handed round plates of thick soup and glasses of star anise, which the guests had no trouble emptying. They had a grudge against her. Why had she come back to the Walbergs? Was she intent on getting her share of the inheritance?

The following morning the rain intensified. The wind got up and carried off the roofs of the cabins in the outlying districts. This time five children drowned in the canal playing with their raft. Despite the terrible weather, in the afternoon the funeral cortege stretched as far as the eye could see. In a church filled to bursting, the priest showered with praise a man who had done nothing but earn money in the least creative way. Then the congregation set off for the cemetery. At the back of the funeral cortege, Auguste could be seen. He had not heeded Jeanne, who had refused to attend the funeral, but did not want to get himself noticed.

The death of Boniface created a gulf between Victoire and Jeanne that was never bridged. Victoire held a grudge against Jeanne for not being present either at the wake or discreetly at the funeral, like Auguste. She especially held a grudge against her for having demanded a certain behavior that was perhaps responsible for his suffering. When she thought of his solitary agony, she could not forgive herself for letting her daughter dictate to her such loathsome behavior. For letting herself be intimidated by reprimands that after all made no sense. What did Jeanne have against Boniface? As Anne-Marie never stopped saying, the Walbergs had brought her up. They had provided her with a comfortable roof over her head, food in abundance, and clothes. And above all an education. Was it their fault if they were white Creoles? Who among us choose our color, our parents, or our birthplace? When the will was read, she would have liked Jeanne to be consistent with herself and refuse the gift that Boniface had made her. Jeanne considered the hundred or so francs pathetic and saw it as proof of the contempt in which he held them. He left nothing, not a cent, not a patch of land, a jewel, or a piece of furniture to Victoire, with whom he had slept to his heart's content for over twenty years. To her daughter he left a pittance. She accepted it because she told herself cynically that it was better than nothing from the slave drivers.

When after a two-week absence Victoire made up her mind to return to the rue de Condé, Jeanne did not reproach her for the time spent at the Walbergs. Yet she was secretly exasperated by what she called her morganatic widow's expression. Victoire dressed herself in loose-fitting black, white, and mauve outfits, wore headties around her forehead in the same colors, and spent hours praying in church. In actual fact, Jeanne's irony hid a violent feeling of remorse. She realized too late the extent of the blow she had dealt both Boniface and her mother by separating them by force. She wondered unfairly why in God's name Victoire hadn't rebelled, knowing full well, deep down, that Victoire had never rebelled in her life.

During these tense times, Victoire continued her visits to the Grands Nègres as if nothing had happened. The only change in behavior was that she practically no longer opened her mouth and botched the weekly dinners. The guests politely swallowed the tasteless dishes, wondering what had gotten into the outstanding cook they once knew. One day she served a young rabbit with tamarind and aged rum that was absolutely inedible.

An incident that might seem comical occurred one Friday evening during the course of one of these suppers. While Victoire had disappeared into the kitchen to arrange a dish, Madame Aristophane, who was a bit scatterbrained, asked:

"Jeanne, why is your maman so sad? Who is she in mourning for?"

There followed a deathly silence that Auguste hastened to fill with one of his never-ending anecdotes. Later on, it needed a lot of tact on his part to get Jeanne to forgive the scatterbrain.

"She did it on purpose!" she sobbed. "She asked it on purpose to hurt me!"

The servants took advantage of this newfound freedom to sow their wild oats. A certain Bergette spent her time in a slanging match with her lover in the corridor to the sounds of "slut" and enough kouni à manman aws to make you shudder. To end it all, the lover hit her over the head with a bottle and left her in a pool of blood on the sidewalk in front of the house. Victoire remained passive and indifferent to these dramas.

Day and night alike, she kept turning the same thoughts over and over again in her head. What a belt of corpses she wore around her waist! What evil eye had she been dealt with to lay to rest all those who came into contact with her? Dernier, Alexandre, and now Boniface. When she was little, people at La Treille accused her of being in league with the devil and a bloodsucking *soukouyan*. It was probably true. She looked at herself in the mirror and what was hiding behind her pale complexion, her slit eyes, and rounded forehead frightened her.

Little Auguste, Anne-Marie, and music continued to be her only source of comfort. She could no longer part with the little boy. She had composed a lullaby for him without which he could never get to sleep.

> *Ti kongo a manman*
> *Ola ti kongo an mwen.*

I have no idea what she felt listening to the outdoor municipal concerts because, unlike I could with cooking, I could never imagine what music meant for her exactly. The orchestra from a frigate, *La Minerve*, that had come over from Fort-de-France for an Offenbach festival, performed *The Tales of Hoffmann*, *La Belle Hélène* and once again *The Grand Duchess of Gerolstein*. As for Anne-Marie, she entertained Victoire with her chatter. Anne-Marie had declared war on Boniface Jr. She had got it into her head to have him interned in the Camp Jacob hospital on the pretext of his inordinate fondness for alcohol. A cousin who was on the board of directors was prepared to issue her with a medical certificate. Needless to say, all these endeavors came to nothing. When it came to intrigues, Boniface Jr. won hands down.

When Jeanne told Victoire she was pregnant again, the announcement was greeted with indifference. Victoire's heart was not in it.

Fortunately, Jeanne felt as fit as a fiddle during this pregnancy and did not need Victoire. This time, nothing brought them together. Neither the bush teas, the perfumed baths, the little treats, nor the massages or the caresses. Jeanne, who had gone back to hard-boiled eggs and tomato salad with one or two sardines in oil as a bonus, now slept beside her husband. She valiantly never missed one day of school.

On July 1, 1912, after a delivery that lasted a mere two hours, Dr. Mélas placed in Victoire's indifferent arms her second grandson.

"Yet another boy!" Auguste groaned, who had given up hoping for a daughter.

Patience! His wish would be granted a little over two years later, and the father who had been indifferent to all his children showed a passionate and blind devotion to this baby girl.

The second son, christened Jean, was truly as splendid as a star, like his mother said, light-skinned in memory of his grandmother, with almond-shaped, languishing eyes and well-defined, sensual lips that he embellished later on with a Cuban-style mustache. During his teens he was the darling of the girls and nicknamed Bel Ami by his classmates. Beauty, alas, is not necessarily a synonym for happiness. During the Second World War, when he was fresh out of medical school, former intern of the Hôpitaux de Paris, his promise of a brilliant future was cut short. Jean was arrested by the Germans one evening while returning home to his studio apartment on the rue de Lille. He died of cold and hunger in the concentration camp at Birkenau. Was he in the Resistance? Was his only crime the fact of being black? I have no idea. I know nothing about this brother. All I know of him is a photo, a real one this time, of a young black dandy with a long white scarf wound round his neck, a gray fedora shading his feminine eyes, a cigarette between his fingers, smiling at the wonderful life he thought was waiting for him. The date: July 1932. He was twenty years old.

It was unusual for a woman at that time to leave her young children and travel for pleasure. And yet that is precisely what Jeanne did. During the long vacation Auguste and Jeanne went on the honeymoon they had had to postpone twice. They embarked on the ocean liner for France. They planned to spend two months in the

City of Light and leave their four little boys in the care of two maids and three *mabo* nursemaids under Victoire's supervision. That was when Jeanne discovered the *métropole*.

I do believe that France and Paris were truly the loves of her life. Traveling by train to the Mont Saint Michel, she contemplated in raptures the passing landscape as she pressed her face against the window. In Paris she chose the apartments where we used to spend her annual leave on the basis of the districts with which she had mysteriously fallen in love. She had a particular fondness for the seventh arrondissement and Saint-Germain-des-Prés, where we stayed on several occasions.

EIGHTEEN

Victoire had lost all willpower.

The house was in a state of plunder. The servants carried off under her nose the barrels of lard, the salted codfish, the smoked herring, the rice and red beans that Auguste had packed in the storeroom in anticipation of his absence. The children went unwashed until noon. Left in soiled baby clothes, Auguste Jr. and Jean had their buttocks covered in rashes. One afternoon when the entire household was on the Place de la Victoire, thieves went into action and boldly carried off furniture and carpets. Something quite unheard of!

This resulted in a raid by the gendarmes in a respectable neighborhood, preoccupied by its image, which did not help Victoire's reputation. Armed with notebooks, they went into every house, using their poor Creole to address the domestics whom they treated as suspects. Worst of all, it became clear that the robbers had benefited from inside help. They arrested two nursemaids, Gazelle and Priame, who quickly made a confession.

Anne-Marie, who saw the mess in which her friend had got, invited her and the boys to come and stay in Vernou. She would be helped by Délia and Maby, whom she knew from the past. In addi-

tion to the change of air, she would be perfectly safe. Victoire preferred to decline the invitation, though she was tempted to accept.
She was afraid of Jeanne's reaction when she learned that her children had found refuge, even temporarily, at the Walbergs. She let
Anne-Marie leave with Valérie-Anne and remained stoically behind
in La Pointe, where the sky and the sea were swollen equally with
bile during this unbearable and suffocating season. The days followed one after another, each one more dismal than the one before.
When she walked over to the Place de la Victoire she was deprived
of the company not only of her alter ego, but also the music. In July
and August the municipal bands took their vacation. She therefore
walked around the square all alone, sat down on a bench on the
Widows' Path, and stared glumly at the horizon. She would return
to the rue de Condé when the first streetlamps were switched on,
for we should point out that at the time La Pointe was no longer a
dark and dangerous place. Even the outlying districts were lit up
thanks to a dynamic new mayor. Dirty tricks could no longer be
hatched in the shadows and there was talk of filling in the stench
from the Vatable Canal. The drainage work, in fact, wasn't to start
until years later. But the town was already being modernized.

Soon, however, passersby noticed a man, a white man, who
would sit down on the bench next to Victoire. He would hold forth,
gesticulating as he discoursed, while she remained silent as usual.
Around seven thirty they would stand up, she tiny beside him, who
was tall and thin, leave the square, and walk up the rue de la Liberté.
Inquisitive bystanders nudged each other in amusement when he
kissed her hand in farewell under M. Bartoleo's balcony.

Who was this man?

We must confess that it was a strange case. The gendarme Antoine Deligny had successfully conducted the investigation on the
burglary of the Boucolon house, rue de Condé. Fifteen years of living in Guadeloupe had given him a sixth sense and without encoun-
tering any opposition he had laid his hands on the crooks in a few
days. They were a gang he had had his eyes on for some time. They

holed up in one of the hovels on the edge of the canal. Their leader was called Isidore Gwo Siwo. Antoine Deligny was a singular man, of an unusual appearance. He was almost six feet six inches tall, still young, forty, forty-five, with a mop of icy white hair covering the top of his head. His metallic blue eyes looked right through you. A few years earlier he had had the immense grief to lose both his wife and his two sons, carried off by an epidemic of typhoid fever. The reason he stayed in La Pointe was because he could not resign himself to leave behind their graves, which he decorated daily with white lilies and purple heliotropes. In the case in question, I can but hazard a guess, since I have been unable to untangle the truth. Was grief the common factor for drawing Deligny and Victoire to each other? Deligny was apparently adept at spiritualism. He turned pedestal tables and communicated with his departed. In this way he said he was capable of conversing with his wife, who even went so far as to write him love letters that he carefully kept in a drawer under lock and key. Did he assure Victoire that she too could see again those she had lost? Did he soothe her nagging remorse regarding Boniface's death? Was that the real reason for her frequent visits to the gendarmerie after daily mass? Antoine Deligny was comfortably housed on the second floor of the police station opposite the church of Saint-Pierre and Saint-Paul: an office, three rooms, a bathroom with a large tub and a shower, a kitchen, and a store room. One of these rooms, filled with tables, chairs, and mirrors, was out of bounds because it was here the séances took place.

I have roamed around the police station quite a bit, hoping in vain to obtain some explanation. Unfortunately, too many years have passed. The gendarmes themselves have changed and darkened in skin. Many young Guadeloupeans now choose to become gendarmes the way they join the state security police force—in order to escape unemployment.

These rendezvous on the Place de la Victoire and visits to the gendarmerie had been going on for some weeks when the SS *Isaura* moored alongside the quay. Jeanne was back, exalted by the marvels of Paris, whose memory still haunted her. Never had La Pointe seemed to her so small and mean. She and Auguste had attempted to decipher the *Mona Lisa*'s smile in the Louvre. They had even traveled to Chartres by train to admire the cathedral's famous angel. After having heard the habanera from *Carmen* so many times, Jeanne had dragged Auguste to the opera. But they had both been bored to death. The love of José for his cigar worker had left them cold. Jeanne had brought back four trunks full of clothes, toys for the children, and records for Victoire: *The Barber of Seville, The Sicilian Vespers,* and *Rigoletto* as well as rugs, paintings, and ornaments for her house, which had acquired the reputation of being one of the best decorated in La Pointe, years before the one on the rue Alexandre-Isaac. Her mother seemed to be in better shape than when she left. Relaxed. Less pale. Almost smiling. The perfect grandmother. She tenderly helped Auguste take his first steps along the balcony and lulled Jean to sleep.

Alas, some good souls, who did not dare approach Jeanne, took it upon themselves to inform Auguste of the reasons for this metamorphosis and made no secret of their comments.

"It hasn't been six months since she buried Boniface Walberg! And already she's seeing someone else! If she hasn't a heart, at least she should behave herself!"

Deeply upset, Auguste waited three days before he picked up courage to tell Jeanne, who couldn't believe her ears. A gendarme! In order to understand their reaction, we must bear in mind what the gendarmes represented in the social hierarchy of the time. The gendarme was the very opposite of the white Creole and the most vile and despised category, the last rung on the ladder: a martinet who does the colonizers' dirty job. The fact that Victoire, after Boniface, had teamed up with a gendarme betrayed an uncommon wish to hurt both her daughter and son-in-law. It was also a sign of perversion. The enormity of the accusation stunned Auguste. He had started to assume his role of extinguishing the home fires and refused to fully believe in such an accusation.

"Ask her," he advised. "Let her speak. See what she has to say."

Jeanne went straight for it, head down.

Personally, I remain convinced that there was nothing between Victoire and Deligny but the séances, the invocations to the deceased, and words of comfort on his part. In my opinion, they shared solitude and grief, not sensuality. Victoire, then, was almost forty years old. An ancestor, an old woman for her time. The time had not yet come when people got married with one foot in the grave. Jeanne was so easily duped and so quick to swallow the slander because, deep down, she had always considered her mother a sort of Jezebel. I think that, beside herself with anger, she lost all sense of proportion and Victoire, as usual, did not defend herself. It was the final split between the two women. And it was never to mend either.

Antoine Deligny exited the picture in January 1913, after a last mass for his dearly departed at the church of Saint-Pierre and Saint-Paul, when he sailed back to France on the SS *Canada*. He retired to Trouville-sur-Mer, where he was born. I know that he wrote the text for a collection of watercolors entitled *Gendarmes in Guadeloupe: The Colony at the Dawn of the Twentieth Century*. I have been unable to find a copy of the book, but during one of my visits to my friend Letizia Galli, who lives in the apartments of Les Roches Noires, I discovered while nosing around the museum with her that a certain Antoine Deligny had worked as a guide during an exhibition of the painter Eugène Boudin, one of whose works was *On the Beach at Trouville*. The museum employees were both intrigued and helpful and gave me the address of the house where he had lived around 1920. I rushed over to find that it was now a pharmacy and nobody could recall anything about him.

After Antoine Deligny left for Trouville, life in La Pointe resumed its former color.

The only difference being that Victoire no longer cooked.

Not only did she no longer set foot in the little outhouse at the back, but she lost interest in everything, she who used to sniff the meat and fowl for hours, inspect the gills of the fish, and scrape the yams to judge the whiteness of their flesh.

I don't think it was a deliberate refusal on her part. It would be difficult to imagine a writer mutilating herself and renouncing her gift on purpose. The gift of writing deserts her, leaves her devastated like the shore after a tsunami. Suddenly, sounds, images, and smells no longer secretly speak to her in a language that only she can decipher. What I mean is that if Victoire no longer cooked, it didn't mean she was rebelling against Jeanne or against society in general. It was the consequence of the loss of her creativity, the result of an immense weariness and a pernicious feeling of what's the use.

JEANNE WAS SO absorbed by correcting her pupils' homework, preparing her lessons, paying visits to the Grands Nègres, worrying about decorum, and caring for her children that first of all she didn't notice. It was Auguste who had to tell her. Hadn't she noticed? Her mother no longer did absolutely anything. The week before, she had been unwell for the weekly reception and they had had to make do with Gastonia's cooking. Wouldn't the same thing happen for the next board of directors' dinner? Shouldn't they ask her what was worrying her?

Jeanne began by answering in no uncertain terms that her mother was not a cook at his beck and call and consequently, she was free to do as she pleased. Then she suspected that this change of behavior could have some worrisome significance. She therefore dashed into the room where Victoire, who stayed in bed later and later, was still lounging between the sheets.

How thin she had gotten these last few months! My God, what had she been thinking? The person she loved most in the world, even though she expressed it so badly, was wasting away and she had not even noticed it! Her skin was diaphanous and her sticky, patchy hair floated like dead seaweed over her shoulders. All the love she felt toward her surged back to her heart, flooding her with its burning wave. She sat down on the bed beside her and took her hand.

"*Ka ki ni?*" she asked softly.

What was wrong? Victoire shrugged her shoulders and played down her condition.

She was tired, that's all. A weariness that tied her down from morning till night. She had lost all willpower. If she were to take her own advice, she wouldn't get out of bed the entire day. Yet she categorically refused to send for the doctor. What she needed was rest. Nothing but rest. And more rest.

Jeanne was perspicacious enough to clearly see the first signs of depression, even though she refused to acknowledge the cause. Constantly accused, victimized, bullied, and prevented from enjoying what in Victoire's own eyes could have lit up her life—love, friendship, and remembrance of lost ones—Victoire was losing her footing. With the energy she was known for, Jeanne undertook to care for her mother. In order to do so, she established a drastic set of rules. She gave orders to the servants that the children were not to disturb Victoire. Especially Auguste, to whom Victoire gave everything he wanted. The result was that she made two people unhappy instead of one. Deprived of his grandmother, poor pasty-faced Auguste whimpered from morning to night and began to regress. He antagonized the servants, who called him all sorts of names:

"*Tèbè! Kouyon! Sòti là!*"

They reserved their adoration for Jean, the little rascal, who walked, stumbled, fell, and bruised himself all over, treating his brother with the contempt that God reserves for inferior creatures.

Before leaving for the Dubouchage school, Jeanne made sure that Victoire's breakfast tray was well stocked with coffee, coconut cassava cakes bought straight from a shop in the outlying district, soft-boiled eggs, and fresh fruit. Several times during the course of the morning she was tempted to leave the class and run back to the rue de Condé. Her sense of duty forbade it and she dispatched two trusted pupils who came back with a detailed report.

"Blood pressure 110 over 80, miss."

"She hasn't got a temperature, miss. It's 98.6 Fahrenheit."

When she came home for lunch she expected to find Victoire in her rocking chair, her back resting on a pile of cushions. Forbidding her to confront the perils of the stairs, she had Victoire's meals sent up to her. Then she enclosed her under her mosquito net for a long siesta. So as to occupy her, she brought her piles of illustrated albums, which Victoire looked at with Auguste, who managed to slip in and join her. Pictures illustrating the tales of Grimm, Andersen, and Perrault. She took pity on the little match girl and admired Karen's red shoes, which reminded her of Thérèse Jovial's present. But the picture she preferred above all was the wolf disguised as the grandmother in "Little Red Riding Hood." Auguste and she reveled in its big gleaming eyes behind spectacles, its large pointy ears under its nightcap, and its sharp teeth sticking out of its mouth. There was only one point on which Jeanne never managed to impose her will. Around four in the afternoon, Victoire flouted all restraints, got dressed, and, as best she could, dragged herself to Anne-Marie on the Place de la Victoire as if it were a salutary recreation.

Times had changed. As a result of deep budgetary cuts, there were no more municipal concerts. Only the bands from the ocean liners moored at quay performed from time to time. The one from an Italian ship, the SS *Stromboli*, gave a performance of *The Barber of Seville* in magnificent costumes.

Yet in the eyes of Victoire, Anne-Marie, who could no longer fit into her dresses, was still just as entertaining as ever. She never stopped talking about her children. A certain Maximilien du Veuzit, a lad of seventeen, the only son of a white Creole from the region of Saint-Claude, who had had the rich idea of exchanging his coffee plantations for banana groves, had noticed Valérie-Anne at an afternoon birthday party and ever since had been languishing for her. In order to leave her mother and the rue de Nassau, Valérie-Anne would have given herself to the devil in person if he had wanted her. Consequently, she too claimed to be lovesick.

Should she let them get married?

Without stopping, Anne-Marie became venomous.

"Give me some news about Jeanne."

She had added some new grievances. Apparently she too had frequented Antoine Deligny's spiritualism séances. Not to get in touch with Boniface, whom she had seen enough of while he was alive, but to communicate with her mother and above all her beloved Etienne, who had passed away accidentally the year before. She had been outraged by Jeanne's accusations. Especially the way she had treated the gendarme. According to her, Jeanne had sent a series of letters denouncing him to the assistant governor general, which accounted for his expulsion from the colony. This seems to me most unlikely. At the time, Jeanne had no access to colonial administration circles. I would even say that as an educated black woman she was automatically suspect. The French authorities had not yet cataloged her among the totally inoffensive, right-thinking personalities whom they showered with republican decorations such as the Palmes Académiques, the Ordre du Mérite Social, and, what was the crowning achievement for my father, the Chevalier de la Légion d'Honneur. Yet as I have said, I have not managed to shed any light on this mysterious affair. Anything, therefore, is possible.

Given her state of health, Anne-Marie would accompany Victoire back to the corner of the rue de Condé and the rue de la Liberté, but not a step farther. She would only set foot in Jeanne's house once Victoire was really sick and bedridden.

Because of this drastic agenda, life on the rue de Condé became even less enjoyable. In the evening, the children, educated as Europeans, were sent to bed very early. The *mabos* left as early as six in the evening and the servants a little later, after they had served supper. Auguste would then read his newspapers, with a preference for *Le Nouvelliste* and its editorials. Sitting opposite him, Jeanne would prepare her lessons and begin carefully correcting the pile of homework. Around nine o'clock she would go up to tuck in her mother, who was listening to records on her gramophone, a present from Boniface. It took all her self-control not to burst into tears and shower her with kisses on seeing how frail her mother had become. Instead, she turned down the lamp on the bedside table, for economy's sake. Shadows stretched over the walls and the tropical night, the color of Indian ink, took possession of the room. Victoire often listened to her records far into the night. She was oblivious to the fact that the sounds carried on the night air and seeped through the persiennes shutters amidst the silence of the street.

"Ka sa yé sa?" the neighbors asked, perplexed.

Music is meant to stir the blood and deliver electric shocks to the heart, the belly, and the sex. It's meant to stiffen your calves with pleasure and set you dancing.

Ah! The Boucolons were a funny lot!

NINETEEN

Valérie-Anne was married one Sunday in August 1914, at La
Regrettée on her father-in-law's estate in Matouba.

War had just been declared in Europe. The majority of Guadeloupeans, however, did not know or did not care. They did not know
it would be so deadly and that so many of them would leave to lose
their lives there.

Despite her failing health, Victoire did not hesitate for one moment. Showing initiative for the first time in her life, she did not
ask Jeanne for permission to leave La Pointe. Jeanne had to accept
the fait accompli when two days before the wedding, very early in
the morning, the Cleveland came to pick Victoire up on the rue de
Condé.

They stopped to buy gas at the Shell gas station, the only one
on the island. Located in the harbor so as to refuel the first motor-
ized boats and automobiles, it caused a sensation. Bystanders spent
hours admiring the mechanized pumps and the attendants in their
red and white uniforms with a shell spread across the middle of
their backs. Victoire sat next to Jérémie, the chauffeur, so as to let
Anne-Marie spread out her weight in the back. He spoke to her with
familiarity, like someone of the same social status. Had she been

following the massive strikes that had shaken the sugar industry to its core? Ah, those needy *maléré* who up till now had been reduced to silence with a plateful of calalu were realizing their strength. They were becoming a proletariat with a formidable force. Victoire did not know what to say. She realized to what extent she was nothing but a leftover from the old days. The modern words were "labor unions," "strikes," and "demands." Jérémie told her there had been a union for domestics for some years. She should have joined. You have to defend yourself since black or white, the boss is the same. A rich mulatto is a white man. A rich black man, a mulatto. The only concern of either is to exploit the weakest.

Bewildered, Victoire was hearing this type of discourse for the first time. I wonder what she thought about it. Did she fully understand it?

Neither she nor Anne-Marie had ever gone farther than Petit Bourg when they stayed at Vernou. Very soon, they found themselves indisposed by the bumps and jolts of the automobile to pay attention to the picturesque landscape. Yet the sight was not to be missed. To the right, villages perched in the opaque green of the foothills. To the left, the blue of the ocean dotted with little white specks of foam. Soon Anne-Marie was snoring. She only woke up when they reached Dolé-les-Bains, where, because of its reputation, she insisted on having lunch.

The spa at Dolé-les-Bains was the first to attract tourists to Guadeloupe. Cubans—recognizable more than anything else by their enormous Havana cigars and bicolor leather shoes—and all sorts of Europeans, French, English, Dutch, and Swedish fought over the rooms in its five-star hotel. From the restaurant guests enjoyed an unobstructed view of the islands of Les Saintes. A sophisticated personnel, trained in Haiti, officiated. While Victoire, as usual, merely nibbled at her food, Anne-Marie ate too much. She helped herself twice to the excellent thrush pâté, the crab *matété*, and above all the chocolate-flavored coconut flan. Around two o'clock they resumed their journey to Basse-Terre. It was the first time either of them had set foot in the capital, since they had never paid Jeanne a visit while she was a student at Versailles. The town was cool, bourgeois, and peaceful. The authorities constantly compared it to La Pointe: "Here, there is a sense of calm," the governors wrote. "It is crime free and trials take place without incident."

Both women were impressed by the battalion of ships waiting offshore to be loaded, by the tamarind trees on the Cours Nolivos, and, above all, the imposing silhouette of the volcano La Soufrière in the distance. The threatening smoke from the fumaroles twirling up into the sky reminded Victoire of the Montagne Pelée and recalled in her heart the happy stay in Saint-Pierre, Martinique, which she had erased from her memory as if it were taboo. Soon, Anne-Marie complained that the air was becoming increasingly cooler as they approached Matouba and they had to stop the car and look for a shawl in the trunk. Uttering cries of fright, she was terrified when the car set off along a winding, mountainous road that threatened to be swallowed up by a dense vegetation of giant red and white dasheen leaves, breadnut trees, all sorts of palms, and the foliage of the ubiquitous lofty tree fern. Jérémie was chuckling to himself.

The estate of La Regrettée was spread over 187 acres and numbered over six hundred coffee trees, which the farm workers were beginning to cut down since coffee was no longer profitable. Bananas were said to have a promising future. If the weather had been more pleasant, the place would have been splendid. But the sky weighed low and gray. The Du Veuzits welcomed Anne-Marie effusively and accommodated her in one of the best rooms in the Great House, whereas Victoire, like Jérémie, had to be content with a bed in the former drying house, converted into a dormitory for the servants. She did not think of it as a humiliation. If she felt morose, it was not because of the ambiguous mistress-servant position, which had long ceased to bother her. It was because suddenly the landscape was so like Saint-Pierre in Martinique that she couldn't get the memory of Alexandre out of her head. As if the past were shaking up his ashes and coming back to haunt and burn her.

The next day was bustling with activity. Victoire would have preferred to stay in the gardens at La Regrettée, where some magnificent Malabar glory lilies were growing. Instead, she had to follow the intrepid Anne-Marie, who had herself driven to the Bains Jaunes, thus named because their waters were strongly mixed with sulfur. A paved road, called the Pas-du-Roy, leading to the baths was unfit for cars but fairly easy for walkers. They had barely returned to La Regrettée when the rain that had been threatening since morning came down in fury. The wind then joined in and it was as if hordes of neighing horses were being whipped as they galloped around the Great House. This lasted the whole night long.

On the day of the wedding, the sun rose radiant.

Three hundred guests—some had come from Martinique and even Puerto Rico, where the du Veuzits had family—squeezed into the former coffee plantation house. Everyone agreed that Victoire was not looking well and seemed sad. Living with her daughter did not suit her! Not surprising! Jeanne was an ungrateful person who was now bad-mouthing religion. (Jeanne had just written that article on teaching in *Trait d'Union* that I have mentioned.) The nuns at Versailles had taken offense and interpreted it as an attack against their teaching methods. The guests also regretted the absence of Boniface Jr. Anticipating a fad that was later to thrive among the middle classes of Guadeloupe and Martinique, he had given as an excuse a hunting trip to the game-rich forests of Haiti that had not yet been felled by the Haitian peasants. On the other hand, everyone was touched by the young bride. Under her bonnet and veil, she looked rather like a first communicant.

"Qué linda!" the matrons of Puerto Rico exclaimed in tears.

As is always the case with weddings, it reminded them of their youth, the time of illusions when the assiduous suitor had not yet metamorphosed into a fickle husband. They got worked up, emotionally imagining an innocent and virginal Valérie-Anne, whereas the cunning little minx, taking advantage of her chaperone's inattention, had arranged on several occasions to taste the forbidden fruit.

When Valerie-Anne had tenderly placed her head on Victoire's shoulder and begged her to take charge of the wedding banquet, Victoire hadn't dared tell her the truth. How could she confess she was henceforth incapable of cooking? Now that she had her back to the wall, in order to create an illusion, she had surrounded herself with a regiment of dark-skinned coolies with oily hair and red dots in the middle of their foreheads who could barely understand Creole since they came from Bombay, Calcutta, and Madras. We should mention in passing that because of this Indian domesticity, the du Veuzits proclaimed they had never enslaved any blacks and had nothing to do with slavery. This did not prevent Jean-René, one of Valérie-Anne's sons and president of the banana planters' union, from being assassinated in 1995 by his plantation workers, who had had enough of him. Victoire was back again amid the smell of browned pork crackling, stuffed fowl, braised lamb, chives, garlic, and spices. But she neither created nor invented anything new. All she did was reel off old recipes to these docile flunkies, more used to throwing together curried *colombos* than perfecting culinary feats—like a novelist who shamelessly uses over again the tricks of the trade in her best-sellers. She looked at her hands and the chagrin at having lost her gift weighed her down. Moreover, this wedding constantly reminded her of another: Philimond's. That time too they had carelessly amused themselves in the shadow of a volcano that had taken offense. In its cruelty it had destroyed their society from top to bottom.

When they went to sit down, the maids of honor passed out white rectangular cartons with gold lettering that Anne-Marie, true to character, had had printed. But this time she did not communicate the menu to the press, as if she knew that Victoire's role was a fabrication. In the secret of their hearts, all those who sat down at table were disappointed. Victoire was not in one of her good days, you could sense it. They didn't hold it against her, however. What writer produces one masterpiece after another?

Around five o'clock the wedding couple left for Trois Rivières, where the boat for Terre-de-Haut, an island in Les Saintes, was waiting for them. There they would spend their honeymoon, for Maximilien, although he had been to Venice and Rio de Janeiro, considered the Saintes one of the marvels of the world. Except for a few fishermen, descendants of Bretons, as blond as corn, the island was virtually uninhabited: beaches of white sand, the sea. In other words, paradise on earth! As Valérie-Anne was throwing her arms around Victoire's neck, her "true maman" as she liked to call her, and showering her with kisses, she noticed that her cheeks were soaked with tears.

"You're crying," she exclaimed. "But why?"

Victoire was incapable of saying why.

My theory is that beginning with that stay at La Regrettée, Victoire was convinced there was nothing left for her on this earth, where her life had lost both meaning and usefulness, and she turned to face death.

AT THE RISK of irritating Jeanne, Victoire had to stay behind another week at La Regrettée. It's true it wasn't her fault. She had caught cold and could not leave on the appointed day.

They were strange, the times she spent in the deserted drying house. Only Jérémie stayed behind with her and faithfully brought her grogs and herb teas. He talked to her untiringly of the importance of labor unions and strikes. Thus began an odd friendship. Later on when Victoire was bedridden, Jérémie found his way to the rue de Condé. He would sit down in her bedroom, ignoring Jeanne's snooty expression and suspicious looks since she took him for a nobody—which he wasn't. Jérémie Cabriou, that was his full name, founded a few years later the first unified union of workers in Guadeloupe, of Marxist allegiance. He was also the first to give his political speeches in Creole, something Légitimus and his people, I think, were incapable of doing. To my knowledge he was the only person who offered to teach Victoire how to read and write. But she brushed him aside.

"An ja two vyé à pwézan!"

"Too old!" he protested. "You must be joking!"

He had no idea that something had died in her.

At night the drying house at La Regrettée was left to the racket of the wind. It made a hell of a row, rushing through the corridors, banging doors and windows, mewing as it burst into the dormitory and playing leapfrog over the single beds. Victoire was unable to get to sleep. Her mind, haunted by the fever, relived and dramatized all the quarrels with her daughter, hearing once again all the remarks she had made to her in anger or impatience. Instead of treating them as a banal result of that inevitable conflict of generations that every parent goes through, she loaded them with a formidable meaning.

She believed she understood why her presence on the rue de Condé was causing a growing embarrassment. The more Auguste and Jeanne felt at ease in the circle of Grands Nègres, the more she reminded them of an embarrassing past.

One dream in particular had a lasting impression on her, she who unlike Caldonia never paid any attention to them. She was following Alexandre along a narrow path, uneasy and stumbling over hidden roots. Suddenly he stopped. They found themselves on a plateau, flat as a platform, at the top of La Soufrière. Or was it the Montagne Pelée? Lost amid the smell of sulfur and lightning. In front of them the ocean.

"Don't be long," Alexandre said. "I'll be waiting for you. It's been too long already."

Then he threw himself like a swimmer into the void. She woke up panting. All around her the cavern of the night resounded with the din of insects and the vociferations of frogs.

Yes, what was she still doing on this earth?

Death, if you call her, is always ready to answer "present," that's a fact. She heard Victoire's voice.

Victoire's fever went down, however, and her cough improved under the combined effects of Jérémie's grogs and herb teas, perhaps, and she returned to La Pointe.

Major changes were in the works on the rue de Condé. In October Auguste left his job as principal of the school for boys on the rue Henri IV. The effect of this was first of all a lot of additional work that he hadn't foreseen. Instead of having an easy time of it, taking his time to walk to his office, going out at ten o'clock for a cane juice at La Palmeraie while joking with the owner, M. Carabin, and nonchalantly presiding over the staff meetings and prize giving, Auguste locked himself up the entire day in a stuffy building on the rue Gambetta and often worked late into the night. Since dividends were still limited, there were no more lavish receptions awash in fine wines. Once a week, the directors of the Caisse Coopérative des Prêts squeezed into the living room, which they filled with thick smoke. When midnight caught up with them, heads lowered over their calculations, they snacked on codfish sandwiches and beer bought from the local corner store.

On Thursday afternoons, however, Jeanne started to receive her friends.

This initiative was much criticized. It was seen to be proof of her megalomania exacerbated by her husband's improved status. She showed off. She played the role of wife of a bank director, a role that the modest Caisse Coopérative des Prêts had difficulty filling. What nobody knew in fact was that she was merely obeying Auguste, who blamed her for being too solitary, too secretive, and encouraged her to become a socialite. My mother obeyed, but she never had any friends. She was too hypersensitive, touchy, hurt, tormented, and offended by teasing or a joke that was perhaps in bad taste but quite harmless. She took offense at the slightest remark and harbored resentment over trivialities. Her bruised and wounded soul never healed.

Once a week she docilely opened her door to the elementary school mistresses of her age and class who talked, laughed, and dressed alike. They were all fond of the same dark fabrics in reaction against the vulgar flowery dresses and straw-colored moleskin hats. All of them showered her with smiles to her face. All of them bad-mouthed her behind her back. In next to no time, she was already a character around whom swirled numerous stories, be they true or false.

She was constantly blamed for the same things, for being arrogant, irascible, and selfish. Taking sides with the Walbergs, somewhat suspiciously, people also called her ungrateful. And finally they accused her of being insensitive and heartless, taking as an example the way she treated her mother.

These ladies ate coconut sorbet in silver bowls and nibbled on madeleines. They pretended to scorn the slander and mainly talked about their classes. Admittedly they were a studious group. That's how they edited *Les Cahiers du Patrimoine,* a series of booklets designed to teach natural science that cataloged local trees and plants together with their medicinal properties. For the time it was considered revolutionary. They were thus rivaling with the aristocracy of white Creoles and mulattoes who believed they had the monopoly on such charitable works. My mother began to demonstrate that generosity which together with her religious devotion soon became excessive, as if she was hiding something in her heart that she was constantly atoning for. At the end of her life she would hand out indiscriminately money and food to needy mothers who, fawning and insensitive to ridicule, called her Saint Jeanne of Arc.

The spitefulness that never left her in peace suggests that during these visits by her "friends" she forbade Victoire to appear, ordering her to stay in her room. Nothing could be farther from the truth. Like on the visits to the Grands Nègres, it was Jeanne who forced her to be present, to eat sorbet like the rest, and smile. She didn't seem to realize that this was torture for her mother. Victoire had her explanation for this, which deep down I share with her. Jeanne was so keen to allay suspicion and convince everyone that she was not ashamed of her mother, whom she paradoxically loved more than anything in the world, that she became tyrannical and cruel.

In short, we might say that with every passing day Victoire was firmly convinced of her uselessness. Caring for the children could have consoled her. But they were being taught to sing *"Frère Jacques"* and *"Savez-vous planter les choux?"* Jeanne was intent on showing they had "good" manners. What was the use of this Creole-speaking, illiterate grandmother?

One Thursday, Jeanne managed to drag her to see Dr. Mélas, who got on well with her. But he was an obstetrician; in other words, he was capable of giving a wrong diagnosis in fields different from his own. As a consequence, Jeanne never forgave herself an act of thoughtlessness that as a woman of extremes she described as criminal. Because of this, she bore a grudge against the doctor and broke off all relations with him. After a perhaps superficial examination, he believed Victoire was suffering from a "pernicious anemia." Her heart, liver, and kidneys were functioning normally, he assured her. Her blood pressure was a bit low. He therefore prescribed some iron in the form of tiny black pills, of which Victoire had to swallow twelve three times a day. With the iron, the affection of her daughter, and that of her grandchildren, everything would soon be back to normal, he concluded jovially.

This was not to be the case. Just the contrary. In the course of the following months, Victoire's health deteriorated to such an extent that she had trouble climbing two stairs on the staircase. She lost weight and weighed eighty-eight pounds, no more than a child. Jeanne was now worried sick. She was prepared to follow the most ludicrous advice. Someone spoke highly of the beneficial effects of the sea, although thalassotherapy was not yet in vogue. Straightaway, she began looking for a rental at Bas-du-Fort or Le Gosier. Though she never missed a day of school, her idea, proof of how worried she was, was to take a leave without wages in order to look after her mother. But Victoire didn't want to miss her daily rendezvous with Anne-Marie. Since an acquaintance had mentioned to her a masseuse who did miracles in Le Lamentin, Jeanne was prepared to drive Victoire there. But since the masseuse demanded half a dozen candles and a yard of white percale, Victoire objected that as a God-fearing person, she did not want any part in magic.

It was then that Dr. Combet arrived from Lille.

He was not a Grand Nègre. He was blond, almost red-haired, with blue eyes. His practice was located on the Grand'Rue in an elegant building not far from the house of Eugène Souques, the actual Saint-John Perse museum, and surprised the inhabitants of La Pointe by making his staff wear face masks. He himself wore a genuine astronaut's outfit: boots, goggles, and a strange uniform covered in pockets. His wife came from Buenos Aires. In short, he seemed to embody the ostentation of the mulattoes. Nevertheless, Victoire's health was reason enough to bend the rules and Jeanne quickly went for a consultation. Something unusual for the time and which added to his prestige, he did not risk a diagnosis before conducting a series of examinations and laboratory tests. For weeks, then, Victoire had to climb docilely up the hill to the hospital, accompanied by Jeanne. She filled vials of blood and urine. Spit into flasks. Gave stool samples. Let them X-ray her organs.

One morning Jeanne and Victoire returned to the Grand'Rue, where Dr. Combet told them in a hushed voice:

"It's leukemia."

What terrified Jeanne was the expression on this man of science's face. Slumped in his chair, he stared at her in awful seriousness. Her intuition told her that very soon she was going to face that moment which terrifies every one of us: the death of one's mother.

TWENTY

I n those days they didn't really know how to treat leukemia.
At the very most they gave Victoire regular blood transfusions.
Surprising as that may seem, the treatment first of all appeared to
work. She gained weight. The color came back to her cheeks. She
sang for her beloved grandson:

> *Là ro dan bwa*
> *Ti ni on joupa*
> *Pèsonn pa savé ki sa ki adan*
> *Sé on zombie kalenda*

By the way, this preference for Auguste irritated Jeanne. She
saw there evidence of her mother's elusive character and her faculty, under her submissive and subordinate airs, to do just as she
pleased. She wouldn't admit it, but Jeanne was jealous of her own
child. Had Victoire felt the same way about her?

When Victoire gained ten pounds, she found renewed hope. Once
a week Victoire went to see Dr. Combet for tests, which he assured
her were satisfactory, and she returned home in good spirits.

At the Dubouchage school, Thursday afternoons were reserved for the "open air." Jeanne led her fifth-year pupils to Bas-du-Fort. All along the two-mile ramble, the mistress and her pupils aroused the admiration of bystanders. Jeanne for her elegance and bearing—"Such a handsome woman," they whispered invariably—the children because they marched in rhythm to songs they shouted at the tops of their voices:

> A kilometer on foot,
> Wears out, wears out
> A kilometer on foot
> Wears out your shoes

Or else:

> One more ki-ki
> Ki-lo-lo
> Kilometer
> One more ki-ki

Every week Jeanne would now drag along Victoire, stubbornly trailing at the back of the group, so that she could fill her lungs with the sea air. It was the time when bathing started to become fashionable. The Guadeloupeans were beginning to appreciate the splendors of their beaches. The children in their panties cheeped and splashed about without venturing too far from the sand. Jeanne and Victoire did not go swimming. They sat on the beach and, both wincing from the sting of the sun, shared a rubber cushion. Jeanne boldly laid her head on her mother's lap and her love for her welled up and suffocated her. "Why has she always been so cold toward me?" she asked herself. "So distant? So reserved?"

Victoire awkwardly caressed her mop of hair, smoothing out the tiny peppercorn curls around her temples. Everything seemed so peaceful and death so far away. However, if Jeanne imagined that the end was far from Victoire's thoughts, she was mistaken.

One morning, out of the blue, Victoire asked Jeanne to invite Anne-Marie, Valérie-Anne, and Boniface Jr. to lunch on Sunday. Whereas everything prompted her to refuse such a proposition, she did not have the heart to reject it, convinced perhaps deep down that the guests wouldn't come. They hadn't seen one another for years. They no longer pretended to be united. To her surprise, all the guests hurriedly accepted; Valérie-Anne, who was pregnant and coming all the way from La Regrettée, even insisted on bringing her husband, Maximilien. A date was set, therefore, for the following Sunday after the sacrosanct high mass.

I am going to call this meal "The Last Supper."

It could be the subject of a painting with Victoire in the center, surrounded by the people she had cherished throughout her life. But on that particular day she did not simply reunite those who were dear to her before death carried her off. It was her way of writing her last will and testament. One day, she hoped, color would no longer be an evil spell. One day, Guadeloupe would no longer be tortured by questions of class. The white Creoles would learn to be humble and tolerant. There would no longer be the need to set a club of Grands Nègres against them. Both would get along, freely intermingle, and who knows, love each other.

The days preceding the lunch, Victoire went into action. She set off back to the market. Slipping on again her old habits, she bargained hard the price of shellfish and fowl. She did not let herself be fooled about how fresh the fish was or how tender the meat. No need to say that on this occasion she outdid herself. Up at four in the morning, she spent the whole of Saturday and most of Sunday morning in the kitchen, since she wanted this meal to remain a lasting memory on the palate and in the heart. My mother wrote out the menu of this memorable day on one of her exercise books that she carefully kept, scribbled with bits of her diary, memos, class timetables, and her children's height and weight.

Conch and freshwater fingerling pie
Sea urchin chaud-froid
Fatted chicken caramelized in juniper
White rice
Rindless pork with breadnuts
Yam puree
Lettuce salad
Coconut flan
Assortment of sorbets

Plus champagne, Auguste's fine wines, and his excellent Courvoisier cognac.

And it could be said, according to one of his favorite sayings, on that day Lucullus dined with Lucullus.

When it came down the rue de Condé, the Walbergs' Cleveland, although less gleaming, nevertheless caused the usual sensation. To say nothing of its occupants. White Creoles! Two men dressed in grayish beige linen suits, wearing pith helmets. Two women in mutton-sleeved, light-colored dresses, arms loaded with presents for the children. The neighborhood watched them as if they were Martians.

Where were they going?

To the Boucolons! Was Victoire about to pass away? They guessed there must be some sort of reconciliation around her deathbed.

Despite the sadness of the occasion, the meal began quite cheerfully. Auguste and Anne-Marie competed for everyone's attention: the former describing his memories of the Universal Exhibition, which never failed to have an effect; the latter, her years at the Conservatoire in Boulogne. My mother and Boniface Jr. sat staring at each other, paralyzed by the desire to make love to each other. Despite his sulky expression, Boniface Jr. was more handsome than ever, his forehead fringed with a whitish blond lock of hair that his mother accused him of bleaching. Valérie-Anne and her husband sat quietly on the edge of their chairs, Valérie-Anne clutching Victoire's hand and calling her "darling little maman," which made Jeanne furious. When Auguste and Anne-Marie let him get a word in, Maximilien talked of the yacht he dreamed of buying. He would sail to all the islands of the Antilles, one after another.

"We live in the most beautiful region in the world," he declared. "And we don't know it."

This nature lover was to make a name for himself as a photographer and later published illustrated albums with the somewhat weak-sounding names of *The Garden of Islands* and *Discovering Eden.*

Just as she was helping herself again to the rindless pork, Anne-Marie suddenly put down her fork and began to cry: noisy, indecent sobs that shook her like a hurricane shaking a tree. Victoire drew her up close and hugged this ill-assorted friend of hers with whom she had shared everything throughout the years. Valérie-Anne also began crying on Maximilien's chest. Hiding her tears, Jeanne felt a painful feeling of exclusion.

MY MOTHER NEVER spoke to me about Victoire's last months, out of fear, I imagine, of reviving feelings that would have been too painful. She preferred to talk about her third pregnancy—she was pregnant again—which she endured in a state of revolt. Physically, she was bursting with health and had the appetite of an ogre, which Victoire was only too pleased to satisfy. But all she wanted were simple, basic dishes. Nothing too elaborate. Spices such as cumin, coriander, basil, and paprika made her nauseous. She didn't like the mixture of sweet and sour or hot and cold. In order to reestablish communication, Victoire had to abide by her tastes, like an author from the Editions de Minuit who prides herself on writing for Harlequin books. At breakfast, she had to have her cucumber salad and fried fish garnished with capers. For lunch she would eat three good-size red snappers in a court bouillon. One day she devoured a whole roast chicken. She was seized by irrepressible cravings and Auguste had to run from one end of La Pointe to the other looking for crab *matété* at a time when there were no crabs because of the torrential rains that season; orange *shrubb* liqueur when it wasn't Christmas; *féros* when it wasn't the season for avocados. Like a vampire, she developed a craving for blood and ate enormous fried slices sprinkled with parsley. Meanwhile, her skin was becoming velvety. Her hair grew strong from invisible juices and tangled over her forehead. She was lovely and vivacious, walking as far as Bas-du-Fort. According to the shape of her belly, not round like a calabash but pointed like a shell from the First World War, Auguste guessed it would be the daughter he so wanted. Moreover, he had dreamed of his late mother, Célanire Pinceau, who had promised him a surprise. Jeanne begrudged him his good mood just as she begrudged her healthy looks. She could not understand why God in His cruelty had made her body a temple bursting with life, whereas her heart was blackened by death.

At the Dubouchage school, since her mind was constantly elsewhere, preoccupied with Victoire's temperatures, dizzy spells, and falling blood pressure, her class was no longer the model it once was, chosen by the principal to show the inspectors on their tour of the colony. For the first time in her career, she was poorly rated. Her iron fist loosened while her proverbial strictness mellowed. Paradoxically, never were her pupils more disciplined or affectionate. During recreation she dashed back to the rue de Condé. When she returned red-eyed, fifteen, sometimes twenty minutes late, the girls, sitting quietly behind their desks, would be reciting their verb conjugations out loud. Some of them offered her bunches of flowers. Others wrote her poems. I have found some of them carefully handwritten in purple ink on squared paper. I have chosen at random the one signed "To my beloved mistress. Anastasie Bonhome, fifth-year elementary school class."

Mother, do you remember
Your child who loves you
And cannot tell you?
Mother,
Take my hand, my little hand
So that
It will warm your poor heart.

Even her colleagues who were used to making scathing, disparaging comments began to pity her. Some of them claimed that she could not cherish her mother to such a degree and be without a heart.

"A sham!" cried the most hard-core of them. "She's playacting."

Once again, passionate discussions broke out in the shade of the mango trees in the recreation yard about Jeanne Boucolon.

Soon, Victoire was too weak to walk to the Place de la Victoire and Anne-Marie, breaking with habit, had to come to the rue de Condé. Every day she would turn up with her viola, flute, bass guitar, records, and mint candies, fanning herself energetically since, owing to her weight, she was always too hot. Jeanne had trouble putting up with these visits. She was probably jealous. We know that deep down she had always been jealous of all those who were close to her mother: Boniface, Jeanne Repentir, Valérie-Anne, Jérémie Cabriou, and Anne-Marie—especially Anne-Marie, who had stolen Victoire from her since childhood. Now that Jeanne would have liked to be alone with her mother, to finally strike up that difficult dialogue which had all too often been interrupted, Anne-Marie increasingly managed to capture Victoire's attention and force out of her one of those rare, secretive smiles. What could she be telling her? Jeanne wondered, mortified. Nothing very interesting, that's for sure: the latest escapades of Boniface Jr.; of Valérie-Anne's difficult pregnancy. Since Jeanne had no friends, she did not know that friendship is largely based on just that: shared trivialities.

Jeanne, however, thought that Anne-Marie was judging her,

blaming her, and bad-mouthing her. This was true in the past. Now Anne-Marie was too affected by the condition of her alter ego and preoccupied by other concerns. Seeing Victoire leave meant losing whole chapters of her own life. It was as if she too were leaving. She had never experienced anything like it since the death of Etienne.

One afternoon, Anne-Marie appeared at the rue de Condé followed by a servant carrying a heavy box of gospel and blues records, a music that was little known in Guadeloupe at the time and had its origins among the blacks from the Deep South. Jeanne, who was as a rule so impervious to any sort of music and anything that was not French from France, became fascinated by these harmonies from elsewhere. For her they seemed to well up from her own suffering, from deep inside her. I often heard my mother hum: *Sometimes I feel like a motherless child.*

Victoire died at the end of June 1915.

According to legend maintained by Jeanne, before passing away Victoire took the hands of Jeanne and Auguste, who were standing next to each other at her bedside, and murmured:

"Sé douvan zot kale a pwezan. Mwen pé pati." (You go on. I can leave now.)

These prophetic words that seem to come straight out of the manual *The Last Words of Honest Souls* are quite improbable. Crammed with morphine, for the cancer had spread to her bones and she suffered agonies, Victoire probably slipped into the other world without saying a word, without revealing anything about herself, the same way she had lived her life.

Jeanne's grief was without bounds. Even her children's kisses could not console her. Not even God Himself, at whose feet she lost herself in prayer day after day. As the modern saying goes, she never got over it. Her grief went even deeper, owing to the conviction that she hadn't been loved because she had been a bad daughter, who had brutalized Victoire and had not been able to tell her everything she meant to her.

But isn't this the risk we all run when we think of our deceased mothers?

She held it against Auguste for accepting Victoire's death with relative indifference and above all for not helping her build a mausoleum in memory of the deceased. I have already said that it was always most reluctantly that he spoke of her. Apart from the times when he gave himself an imaginary set of parents, he never mentioned anyone. It was quite by chance I learned that his mother, Célanire Pinceau, died accidentally, burned alive when her shack made of old soap boxes went up in flames while he was out playing football near the hospital. As a result, the colonial authorities put him into care and enrolled him in the Lycée Carnot's boarding school. His guardian was a mulatto notary, a fervent churchgoer, to whom his mother had hired her services. I think I am unfair to my father. Too much suffering during his teenage years had stunted his feelings.

In her grief and her remorse, Jeanne constructed a myth that barely corresponded to reality and left in the dark uncertain aspects of Victoire's personality. In short, she endeavored at all costs to have her conform to the clichéd norm of the Guadeloupean matador, the fighting woman who courageously resists life's trials. As for me, I prefer my grandmother to remain secretive, enigmatic, the improper architect of a liberation that we, her descendants, have known how to enjoy to the full.

Two WEEKS AFTER the death of Victoire, amid the popular rejoicing of a July 14 Bastille Day, Jeanne gave birth to a baby girl, who from the very cradle was lovely and melancholic, as if the sorrows of the mother had been passed on to her: my sister, Ena.